by

JIM PAHZ

Lilith is a novella and a work of fiction. Any similarity of the characters to people living or dead is coincidental and unintentional.

The Writers' Collective
Mount Pleasant, Michigan

ISBN - 978-0-9886423-1-7

BOOKS BY JIM PAHZ

Saving Turtles

Lilith

CO-AUTHORED WITH CHERYL PAHZ

Almost Chosen...Nearly Saved

McAngel

Finding Quetzal

Robin Sees A Song

The Last Adventure Box

All books are available at Amazon.com

Male and Female: He created them.

Genesis 1:27

1

It is an eighty-acre parcel, located in the northeast quadrant of Michigan's Lower Peninsula, twelve miles from the village of New Jericho. The land has been in Ryan's family for more than one hundred years. It is mostly wooded and adjoins State land. This part of Michigan is sparsely populated and wildlife abounds.

Today, it is mid-January and it is cold. Normally, on such a day, Emma wouldn't jog. But her husband Ryan, a college professor, is away for three days at a SOPHE conference—the Society for Public Health Education—and Emma is bored. She wants to get her body back in shape, although she doesn't know in shape for what. She thinks, *I am getting older. It's important to keep myself fit.* So Emma changes into her jogging suit, puts on a down vest and a wool cap that covers her ears. She heads for the woods.

She jogs on the path Ryan made for the grandchildren for their 4-wheelers. He made the trail serpentine, and it meanders through the eighty acres that comprise the Dennison homestead. To make the trails, he pulled something called a "drag-harrow" behind one of the 4-wheelers, which completely removed the vegetation and left a terrific path for riding, walking, or jogging. This afternoon, the path is relatively snow-free as the drag has removed the protective layer of leaf litter, and the dark color of the soil has absorbed the heat and melted the fresh snow.

Emma jogs for a quarter-mile through the trees. It is dark and foreboding. The leafless trees seem like skeletons. She feels uneasy and turns her thoughts to her children. She and Ryan have two daughters, Ruth and Jamie. Both have left the nest and are now on their own. Ruth is married to Michael and has two children. They live in Texas. Jaime, the older girl, is much closer to home, living in an apartment in New Jericho. Emma misses the children. The place seems cold and empty, and now, with Ryan away at the conference, Emma feels isolated and she doesn't like that feeling at all.

The property is so remote that jogging through the woods, Emma feels vulnerable. She probably should have stayed in the house and found something to do inside. She senses darkness in the woods. She felt it earlier when she walked down her long driveway to check her mail. But the ominous feeling is stronger now. *What*, she wonders, *is lurking behind the Russian olive?* The plant grows everywhere. Originally it was brought over from Asia in the 1830s, to be used as a windbreak, or for erosion control. Nobody realized back then how invasive the species would become, or how it would undermine native flora. Now the stuff grows all over Michigan and no matter what Ryan or Emma do, they can't eradicate it.

What will be the next invasive species? Emma wonders. Then, the answer comes to her, *Those fish—the Asian carp.* She knows that Michigan is preparing for another onslaught. An all-out state and federal effort is underway to prevent these fish from entering the Great Lakes. An electronic barrier has been installed near Chicago.

Emma imagines an army of carp, silver and bighead, poised to invade the Great Lakes and ruin the waters for sports fisherman. *You can't keep us out!* The fish laugh, as they gather their forces and march in lockstep towards the lakes.

Since it is January, Emma can see a little ways through the bare bushes, and into the distance. This time of the year, the Russian olive doesn't have leaves. Once springtime arrives, the leaves will come back. Then the brush will form an impenetrable wall of foliage. Again Emma wonders, *What is behind the trees and the Russian olive? Is something watching me?* The sky is overcast, blocking out the sunshine—a gloomy day. Emma thinks it likely will snow again later in the afternoon. Talking out loud, to herself, Emma says, "I'm glad Ryan will be home soon. I don't like being out here by myself—it's lonely and just a little scary."

Emma jogs about a half mile when she reaches the center of the property and stands at the edge of the meadow. Looking across the field of grass, Emma sees a dog. It stands motionless watching her. She doesn't recognize the animal. The dog was probably in the woods earlier, when she walked down her driveway to check her mail. She understands now, why she had a sense of foreboding.

It's a big, black-and-tan-colored dog with

semi-long hair. Emma thinks it might be a Collie/Shepherd mix. She can't see if it is wearing a collar, but she is not that close to the dog, and a collar could be hidden by its long hair. Unless.... *Oh my, maybe it's not a dog at all. Maybe it's a wolf. There are wolves in Michigan, but not in this area—are there? There are some not too far away. Wolves have been seen as far south as Cadillac and Gladwin.* Emma panics. She tells herself not to run. *Stand your ground. Be unconcerned. Don't let it sense fear. If you run you will trigger a prey response and it will attack.* Emma slowly kneels down and picks up a tree limb. It is a good, stout branch, about four inches in diameter. Her intention, if all else fails, is to use it like a baseball bat or club.

She rises and begins to back away, slowly, walking the same trail, but in reverse. She keeps her eye on the dog. The animal follows. It moves deliberately, and never takes its eyes off Emma. Gradually it begins to close the gap between itself and Emma. The dog is about ten feet away. It growls, menacingly. She hears the animal and is terrified. In an effort to pacify the creature she begins to talk softly to it.

"Hi fellow, you don't want to hurt me. I am your friend. Can't we work this out?"

The dog lowers its head. It continues growling and looks like it's about to leap. Emma raises the branch and takes a baseball stance. "Oh God," she prays, "protect me." She feels something wet running down her leg, just before she hears the sound of a motor off to her right. The dog hears it too. He turns his head as two 4-wheelers come straight at him. The dog leaps sideways and runs off into the bushes. It makes absolutely no sound. In a moment there is no evidence the animal was ever there.

Two machines ride up on the trail which is perpendicular to the one on which Emma is standing. The vehicles stop. They are being driven by two boys. The older boy looks like a teen-ager. He has a little hair on his chin and Emma thinks he might be fifteen or sixteen years old. He looks familiar. She believes he's been to her house before and thinks he lives in the development east of their homestead. He appears typical in every way. The second boy is smaller and looks younger. His head is perfectly round attached to a fat little body. Emma thinks he is adorable and looks like Humpty Dumpty.

"What happened?" The first boy asks. "Why are you holding that branch?"

"Didn't you see it?" Emma asks, "That dog? It was a big dog. It might have been a wolf. I'm not sure."

"Oh yeah," the first boy replies. "I saw it. I thought it was your dog, like a pet or something. I'm glad we scared it away."

"I'm not so sure you scared it. It was ferocious looking, but it did run off, so you did something. I'm grateful. Do you suppose one of you fellows could give me a ride back to my house? I'm afraid to jog with that beast in the woods." Emma hopes the boys don't realize that she has wet herself. She feels embarrassed, but since her sweatpants are dark blue, she doesn't think they will notice. She will have to risk it.

"Of course," the first boy answered. "Mr. Denninson said we could ride on your trails. They're the best ones around. I hope you don't mind."

"Not at all," Emma said. "My husband is out now, but he'll be back soon. I will tell him how you guys rescued me. I'm sure he'll want to thank you himself. You are heroes. You boys can ride these trails any time you want so long as your parents approve. But I think you should be careful. Get yourself some kind of weapon in case you run into that animal again, and it decides not to run away."

"I have a sling shot," the Humpty-Dumpty-boy said. He held it up for Emma to see.

"That might work," she answers, "but maybe not enough. I think you better talk to you parents about this. And I wouldn't ride alone. Be sure you always have a companion with you."

"Okay," the Humpty Dumpty boy says. "I'll tell my dad."

"How old are you?" Emma asks. "What grade are you in?"

"Ten. I am in the fifth grade."

Emma looks at the little boy. He is so cute she wants to hug him and take him home with her. He has a teddy-bear quality about him.

"Climb on the back of my 4-wheeler" the older boy says. "I'll take you home."

Emma gets behind the boy and straddles the seat. She is still trembling from fright.

"Please go slow," she says, "I am a little frightened of these machines."

"All right," the boy replies. "Don't worry, Mrs. Dennison. I'll be careful." He accelerates the machine and slowly heads back to Emma's house. When they arrive home, she asks the boys if they would each grab a piece of firewood from the woodpile and place it on the front porch by the door. The boys are happy to comply. As soon as they set out to the woodpile, Emma removes her cap and uses it to wipe off the seat. There is no evidence. She is confident that nobody was aware of her accident.

"You boys wait here for a moment." Emma says. "I have fresh cookies inside and I want you to have some. It is my reward to you for rescuing me." Emma goes into the house to fetch the cookies.

Jim Pahz

2

New Jericho is a seasonal community that has a reputation for being an arts center. During the summer, the population triples, as tourists flock to town to visit art galleries, unique shops, and restaurants. The community is quaint and, at the same time, trendy. It is on the must-see list of unique Michigan towns, competing for the tourist dollar with such places as Traverse City, Saugatuck, and Mackinac Island. In addition to its cultural offerings, such as outdoor art shows, community theater, and garden club displays, New Jericho is known for its numerous public parks, clean rest rooms, and outdoor festivities.

In winter, things are different. There are no tourists, and many of the trendy shops in the downtown area are closed. Not all, but most. The central part of town resembles a ghost town, and won't come back to life again until the Waffle Festival in April. The stores on side streets, however, remain open. These consist of a hardware store, a super market, a bakery or two, a discount establishment, a used clothing store run by the Salvation Army, and a couple of franchise restaurants such as Pizza Hut, McDonald's, and KFC. There are also a few art galleries that remain open, those owned by residents who live in New Jericho year round.

Today, it is unusually cold as Emma walks from the delicatessen where she buys the specialty cheese that Ryan likes so much. She puts her few items in her car. It is not a typical winter day, if there is such a thing. There is a strong north wind blowing down from Canada. It's what the weatherman calls a *Siberian Express*. Emma wouldn't have bothered even coming to town on a day like this, but Ryan will be home from his conference tomorrow and she wants a treat for him. So a trip to town is necessary, even though the wind tears through her coat which seems to offer little protection and less warmth. Emma is chilled, but notices that a few doors up the street a person emerges from an art gallery. The sign above the door reads Amanita Gallery. *They must be open,* Emma thinks. *Maybe I'll just go inside, browse and get warm.* She closes the car door and bolts to the gallery.

Once inside, she immediately feels better. The warm air engulfs her and she doesn't feel so frozen. Emma strolls through the gallery. It is not big, consisting of three rooms of varied paintings; some are modern abstracts, while others are realistic renditions of nature scenes. Almost immediately, Emma's eye is drawn to a large painting hanging by itself. Done in oranges and reds, it is a picture of an old, gnarled tree. What is extraordinary is that where the branches end, the tree is budding babies.

Emma is transfixed by the painting. She has never seen anything like it. She hears a voice behind her.

"It's unusual... isn't it?"

Emma turns and sees an older gentleman in a suit and bow tie. He appears awkward, his movements are stiff and he looks pasty, like he needs some time in the sunshine. He offers a forced smile. "It is called *The Tree of Hope*. There is another one with a similar name that hangs somewhere in New York. It might be in the Metropolitan Museum of Art, or at the Guggenheim Museum, I can't recall. I saw it when I was a younger man.

I think that one might have been called *The Tree of Life*. This interpretation is by a local artist."

"It's amazing," Emma says. "I've never seen anything like it. It's so realistic and at the same time disturbing. It really grabs you."

"Yes," the man says. "She's very good. There is another one of her paintings in the other room. Please feel free to wander. If you have any questions or need assistance, just call me. That's what I am here for."

"Thank you," Emma replies. "You say she's a local artist?"

"Yes, that's right."

"Is the picture for sale?"

"No, not *The Tree of Hope*. It's on exhibition only. I wish I could sell it. A lot of people inquire about it. But the old lady is adamant. She refuses to part with it."

"Is that her name—Lilith?"

"Yes, that's correct."

"I would like to meet the artist, especially if she is local."

"I'm sure that would be quite impossible. She is reclusive and very old. She's the only artist I know who genuinely shuns publicity.

I think she hates people."

"How old is she?"

"I don't know, but I would guess somewhere in her 80s, perhaps 90s. She walks with a walker and has one of those oxygen tanks with a tube to her nose. She was probably a heavy smoker in her younger days. I'm speculating, of course. I have only seen her a few times and always on business; never socially."

"Interesting."

"Yes. Go look at her other painting. Her realism is so incredible you would think it was a photograph. It's not; it's the genuine article and, if you look carefully, you can see the brush strokes." The man turned and walked away.

Emma walks to the other room. She glances at all the pictures, her eyes finally coming to rest on a medium-sized oil painting with a heavy, intricately carved, gold-colored frame. The picture is of a woman jogging on a trail. In the corner is the back of an animal's head. It appears to be a wolf—observing the jogger.

"Oh my God," Emma says out loud. A chill runs up her spine and she feels a tingling in her fingers. "It's me. The wolf is looking at me." Emma turns and practically runs out of the gallery.

"Come back again," she hears as she flees the gallery. "It's been a pleasure."

3

When Ryan returned home, Emma embraced and kissed him. "How was the conference in Phoenix?"

"Good."

"I'm so glad you're home," Emma said. "I had an encounter with a wolf."

"What... really?"

"I went jogging two days ago, and when I reached the clearing I saw this animal looking at me. At first I thought it was a big dog. But then I wasn't so sure. It looked like a wolf and it approached me and began to growl. I thought it was going to attack me. I picked up a branch to defend myself, but just then two boys came riding up on 4-wheelers and the animal bolted. I think it was the Patterson boy who lives east of here, and one of his little buddies."

"I know the boy. He's always trying to sell something for his school. He's a nice kid and he asked me if it would be all right to ride our trails. I gave him permission."

"I'm so glad you did. I think without him

I'd be a goner."

"Don't jog in the woods by yourself, sweetheart. Let me check things out. I'll take the shotgun and look for it. Besides, what are you doing jogging in this weather? It's too cold and windy."

"I know," Emma answered. "I don't know what I was thinking. But there's more Ryan! There's an art gallery in town. I went there yesterday, just to get out of the cold. I saw something that sent chills up my spine. It was a picture of a wolf eyeing a jogger in the woods. I think... I think the jogger was me."

"Emma, you're kidding me. I'm sure you can't be serious. Who painted the picture?"

"Someone named Lilith."

"I'd like to see this work of art. Let's go tomorrow. Obviously the painting was done some time ago. Otherwise it wouldn't be hanging in a gallery. The paint was dry, wasn't it? You said your encounter with the wolf was two days ago. The artist would have had to be a mighty fast painter to record the incident, have the paint dry, frame the picture, and hang it on a wall. Wouldn't you agree?"

"I suppose. Unless, of course, she painted

the scene knowing it would happen sometime in the future."

"Emma, listen to yourself."

***

The following morning, when Ryan and Emma went to town, they were in for a disappointment.

"Wouldn't you know it!" Emma turned the door handle one more time. She pushed and pulled at the door. "It's closed, damn it; the gallery is closed. I can't believe it."

"It happens," Ryan said.

"But it was open just two days ago. Who closes their store on a Tuesday?"

"Emma, it's winter and you are in New Jericho. How many paintings do you think they're going to sell on a Tuesday in the middle of winter? The gallery may stay closed until the Waffle Festival."

"I know, but it's just so damn frustrating. I wanted you to see that picture."

"I will, Emma. We aren't going anywhere. I'll see it, just not today. We'll stop by each time we come to town and eventually, one day, the gallery will be open and then I will see the picture of the wolf eyeing its dinner."

"That's not funny, Ryan. I could have been that dinner."

"But you weren't, Emma. That's the point. You're still here. I've spent two hours in the woods and haven't seen that wolf anywhere. If it even is a wolf. You said yourself it might have been a dog. Maybe it was someone's pet that ran away. Who knows? Let's go home, sweetheart. We'll come back in a few days and try again. Let's forget it for a while."

***

During the following weeks, Ryan and Emma returned to the art gallery several times. Each time they stopped, the place was closed. After the last effort, Ryan said to Emma, "Forget about it. Wait until April after the festival and then the gallery will be open. They've obviously decided to close for the winter. That's what most of the businesses here do. You know that. You need to be patient, Emma. Spring will be here before you know it."

"But it was open. I don't understand it. I was there."

"I know, Emma. It was open the day you saw the paintings. But it probably was an exceptional day, an aberration. Maybe they were taking inventory. Who knows? But it hasn't been open since, and we have stopped many times already. Forget about it. April isn't that far away. We'll come back."

"All right. I guess you are right, but it's a hard thing to do. I wanted you to see that painting."

"I know, Emma. Don't obsess over that picture."

"It's not obsessing, I'm just concerned."

"I understand."

Jim Pahz

4

In April the weather turned unseasonably warm. One afternoon, while Emma was in town shopping, she saw an old woman emerge from the gallery. *At last,* she thought, *it's finally open.*

The old woman was pushing her walker and moving slowly. Although she was a half block away, Emma easily caught up with her.

"Excuse me," Emma said.

The old woman didn't acknowledge Emma's presence. She kept walking.

"Pardon me, I couldn't help but notice you came out of the gallery. I've been trying to get in there all winter. I visited once, but every time afterward I found the place was closed. It must have been a fluke or something the one time the gallery was open. Do you think? I hope I'm not disturbing you, but I was wondering, would you be the artist, Lilith? You see, I was very impressed by a painting I saw—well, actually two— and when I inquired about the artist, the proprietor said it was a local artist named

Lilith. I didn't get her last name, but he told me the artist was an elderly woman and she used a walker. So naturally, when I saw you come out of the gallery, I put two and two together and assumed you might be Lilith."

The old woman stopped. She turned her head and looked at Emma. The gallery proprietor had been right when he described the artist. The woman was old. She looked ancient. Her skin was almost translucent and you could see her veins. And she was covered with wrinkles. She appeared extremely frail, and of little weight. Emma could see she needed a walker to anchor herself to the ground. *In a good wind,* Emma imagined, *the old woman could be lifted off the ground and blown away like a leaf—oxygen tank and all.*

The most striking feature about this old woman was her eyes. They were opaque and a pale blue, the color of a robin's egg. Emma thought they must be damaged. The woman probably had cataracts. Emma wondered if the woman could even see her, and assumed the old lady's vision was impaired. But if that was so, how could she paint? Maybe this wasn't the artist, after all. There was something unsettling about the old woman, and seeing those eyes sent a chill up Emma's spine.

"Never assume." The voice was weak and squeaky with a gravel-like quality.

"No... of course not. But I had so little information. You have to rely on the evidence you have, so I assumed, because of your advanced years, that you might be Lilith."

"I might be, if I wanted to say, which I don't."

"I thought you were." Emma was pleased with herself; she felt like a detective who solved a puzzle. "I just want to tell you that your pictures are awesome, marvelous, and I was wondering...."

"I don't give interviews."

"Oh no, of course not. I don't want to bother you, and I'm not asking for an interview. I'm not a reporter or anything like that...."

"Then go away. Leave me in peace." The woman continued to walk down the street.

Emma ignored the woman's request and followed. "I was only wondering.... You see there's this picture you painted. Well, I assume you painted it. A forest scene and there is a woman jogging through the woods.

It looks like…. Maybe I'm crazy, but the woman in the picture appears to be seen from the perspective of an animal—maybe a wolf."

"You peed yourself."

"What?

The woman cackled—a shrill, witch-like laugh. "I could smell your fear." She kept walking, but this time Emma didn't follow. She stood transfixed and watched as the woman moved away from her and continued to walk down the street. Emma had a sick feeling in her stomach and felt weak in the knees. She fought to keep herself from throwing up. *How could she know? I didn't even tell Ryan. I was too embarrassed.*

Driving home, Emma kept going over the episode with the creepy old woman. *How is it possible?* she wondered. *Is the woman a witch? Maybe she is a shape-shifter. What is a shape-shifter? Are there really such things? There has to be some logical explanation.*

When she got home, she told Ryan of the incident.

"Are you sure you heard her correctly?"

"I'm certain."

"It doesn't make sense, Emma. Could

you have imagined it? It was a windy day and maybe you just heard her wrong. Maybe you heard most of what she said, but didn't hear some words and your imagination filled in the blanks. That sort of thing sometimes happens."

"No, Ryan, I heard what she said. I'm certain of that."

Ryan shook his head to clear the cobwebs. "Let me see if I understand you. You were intimidated by an old lady with a walker, who was on oxygen? Is that what I am supposed to believe?"

"I wasn't intimidated by the woman herself; it was by what she said and what she represents."

"And what is that?"

"Witchcraft. Satanism. The black arts. Something of that nature."

"So, the old biddy is a witch. Do you think she rides a broomstick?"

"Ryan, it's not funny. This is serious."

"I'm sorry, Emma. It's hard to take this conversation seriously. Isn't it possible that you imagined the dialogue with this woman? I'm not a psychiatrist, but I know that sometimes the mind plays tricks on people for all kinds of reasons. Maybe...."

"I know what you're going to say. Maybe I'm crazy. Is that it? Is that what you think? Your wife is nuts?"

"No Emma, I don't think you're crazy, but I'm not so quick to write off the artist as a witch or look for a supernatural explanation. We're not in the middle ages. It's the 21st century. Your condition could have an organic cause. Maybe you have a brain tumor, or an embolism pressing on a nerve. Maybe you hallucinated. Maybe, like Ebenezer Scrooge said in *The Christmas Carol,* there was more of undigested potato than anything supernatural. All I'm saying, Emma, is I'm not a medical doctor. More investigation needs to be done. I think we should begin by having you go to a doctor for a complete physical evaluation. Meanwhile, since it is spring and the gallery is now open, we can return and check it out. We can find the artist's name and see where she lives. We'll pay her a visit and see the old biddy in person. We can get some answers and maybe even a painting or two. I mean, if she doesn't cast a spell over us."

Emma could see that Ryan found the

whole thing amusing.

"Whatever happens," he continued, "you will have a witness."

***

The following day, Ryan didn't go to work. He called in sick. Instead, he and Emma went to town and returned to the Amanita Gallery. When they entered, there was a ting-a-ling from a bell which hung on a string.

"Look at this," Emma said. She led her husband to the picture of the tree blossoming babies.

"That's different!" Ryan said.

"Yes, it's incredible. Now come and look at this one." She led Ryan to the adjacent room and scanned all the paintings on the wall. She had a frown on her face when she addressed Ryan. "It's not here. The wolf picture is gone." Raising her voice she yelled, "Hello, is anyone here?"

A man entered from a back room. He was the same man that Emma had met several months ago. She estimated he was about 60 years old. He wore an ill-fitted suit that was long out of fashion. He also had on a white shirt and bow tie. He still looked pasty, and not healthy at all.

"Can I help you?" the man asked.

"I was looking for the picture that hung on this wall in January. It was a picture of a woman jogging through the woods and the artist's name was Lilith."

"If it's not here, it probably sold. I'll check the records in the back and see what I can learn. Excuse me for a moment, please."

When the man turned to go, Emma said, "How could it have sold?" She couldn't hide the annoyance in her voice. "The gallery has been closed the whole winter. Every time I came here, the door was locked."

"I'm sorry for your inconvenience. During the winter months, the gallery is open by appointment only. If I had known you were interested in seeing our works I would gladly have opened the gallery. You had only to call."

"I'm sorry," Emma said. "I didn't think to do that. Could you please check your records?"

"Of course." The man started to walk from the room.

Emma turned to Ryan. "I can't believe it. First the gallery is closed, and now this. I always have the worst luck."

The man returned holding a white index card. "Yes, now I remember the picture. I was correct. The work was sold. It was only a week ago."

"Who bought it?"

"We're not really at liberty to divulge that information. It's policy, you understand." The man lifted his right hand and began rubbing his thumb behind his ear. Then he placed his thumb under his nose and sniffed it. "But I can tell you they weren't from this area. They were just passing through on their way home."

"Home?"

"Yes, they were going back to Massachusetts." The man hesitated. "All right, I guess it would be okay. I mean, I don't see what harm it can do." Again he started rubbing behind his ear. "Since they're not from here." He smelled his thumb again. It was apparently an involuntary response and he wasn't aware of doing it. "Their names were Diane and Carl Wolf."

"Wolf? Did you say their name was

Wolf?"

"I did. Is something wrong? Do you know them?"

"No," Emma said, "I don't know them. I just think it's weird. I mean the painting was a scene from the perspective of a wolf. The animal was watching a woman jog through the forest."

"Oh my, that is a coincidence, and amusing too."

"Isn't it? Listen," Emma said, "I ran into Lilith yesterday. At least I think it was Lilith. I tried to make conversation."

"Oh my, I bet that didn't go well. Did she bite your head off?"

"Almost."

"She's not what I would call a people person, if you get my drift."

"I do, and I agree."

"She doesn't give interviews."

"So I learned. But we left some things unsaid and I really would like to finish our conversation. Could you tell me her name and address?"

"Her name is Lilith. It's right there on the painting."

"I already know that, but is that her first

or last name?"

"To be honest, I'm not really sure. I make her checks out to L. Lilith, so I assume it is her last name. I don't know what the L stands for. She never told me. It's not like we're friends, you know."

"Her address?"

"I really don't feel comfortable giving out that information. I don't think it is appropriate."

"Whatever. But can you at least tell me how to get to her house? I am a potential customer and the customer is always right. I think that's the way it's supposed to be."

"I just don't know if I should…. I might get into trouble. She could take her work to another gallery."

"Come on, risk it. Be bold. It would mean a lot to me. Please? I will tell her I am such an ardent admirer that I pressed you for the information. You fought kicking and screaming—something like that."

"Well… I suppose it wouldn't hurt too much. She lives about twelve miles out of town. Take Highway 33 north, about a half-mile past the Strickland Church. Turn right on Huber Road and go about 2 miles. Her drive is on the left, but I think it's unmarked. It goes a long way, about a mile. It's a private road, just a two-track and very sandy. After a good rain the road is impassable, so be careful. Go when the weather is good."

"Thank you. Thank you very much, Mister... I'm sorry I didn't get your name."

"Metcalf. Jeremiah Metcalf."

"Thank you, Mr. Metcalf."

She and Ryan began to leave the gallery. Ryan stopped to study the picture of the sprouting babies. "That's quite a painting. I've never seen anything like it."

"That's what everyone says. It was done by the same artist your wife is looking for—Lilith."

"Something is different," Emma said.

"What?" Ryan turned to Emma.

"I don't know what it is, but something. I can sense it. It is different than when I saw it last." Emma stared at the painting, puzzled.

"I can assure you," Mr. Metcalf said, "nothing is different. The painting hasn't left our walls."

"I can't put my finger on it, but something has changed. Something is not right."

As Emma and Ryan left the gallery she

noticed one more thing. It was a sign that hung on the wall, just above the thermostat. The sign read, *Please, no photographs.*

When they got into their car Emma asked, "Why do they care if someone takes a picture?"

"Probably because they don't want an amateur painter copying another person's art. It's a matter of pride and ownership. They don't want the work stolen. Things always boil down to money. Somehow I believe money is the cause of their policy."

"Did you see how that man kept rubbing the back of his ear and then smelling his thumb?"

"I did."

"I thought it was gross. I almost said something."

"I'm glad you didn't."

"Yes, I know, he probably would have taken offense. Are we going to look for Lilith?"

"If you're ready. It hasn't rained today. The weather is good and the sand is dry."

"Let's go."

Jim Pahz

5

"Have you ever seen anything as cute as this cottage?"

"No," Emma answered. "It looks like something out a nursery-rhyme book for children. It is adorable. I can't believe it's real."

"Look at the door. It's round on top. When have you ever seen a door like that in Michigan?"

"Never in Michigan. I've only seen those in story books."

"Look at the carved owls on each side of the door."

"Like sentries guarding the house."

"That's what I was thinking. This is not your usual tract home. It's custom designed and built. And I'm guessing it has been here for a long time. I feel like I am in a Disney movie. Maybe a Hobbit lives here. Look there, Emma, the easel. I bet that is where the old lady does her painting."

Ryan approached the door and knocked. Nobody answered. They waited a few minutes and Ryan knocked again. Nothing. They turned to leave and had taken just a few steps when they heard a voice behind them.

"Hi there...." It was a sweet, melodic voice, almost like music. "Can I help you?"

They turned and observed a young woman somewhere between 18 and 25 years of age, dressed in a simple white cotton dress, and wearing leather sandals. She had long black hair that tossed about in the breeze. Her complexion was perfect, without any blemish whatsoever. Her smile was radiant. She held a basket that contained mushrooms.

Noticing the couple staring at her basket, the young woman said, "Morels. I've been gathering the mushrooms. It's that time of the year. They're so yummy. Do you know that if you find a dead elm tree on the ground, that's where you'll find the morels? That's the spot."

"Excuse me," Ryan said, ignoring the girl's question. "I'm Ryan Dennison, Dr. Dennison, and this is my wife, Emma. We don't mean to disturb you. We just came to speak to Lilith."

"Why?"

"It's about one of her paintings."

"Which one?"

Emma answered, "It was a picture of a girl in the forest being eyed by a wolf. At least I think it was a wolf. I suppose it could have been a dog—a big dog, or maybe a coyote? I've never seen one of those. We returned to the gallery yesterday to get another look at the picture but it was gone. Mr. Metcalf said it had been sold, if you can believe this, to a couple named Wolf."

The girl smiled. "You mean to tell me the Wolfs bought the picture of the wolf?" She chuckled. It was a sing-song, melodic laugh. "That is funny. Do you think if the picture had been of a coyote it would have been bought by Mr. and Mrs. Coyote?" She laughed again.

"I couldn't say. Mr. Metcalf also found it funny that the picture was bought by Mr. and Mrs. Wolf."

"He's a sweet man; a little stuffy. I don't think he has much of a sense of humor."

"We don't really know him. Are you familiar with the painting we're talking about?"

"Of course."

"Do you think Lilith will agree to see us?"

"I don't see why not."

"Then you'll take us to her?"

"I don't need to."

"Why is that?"

"You're already talking to her, silly. I'm Lilith, but you can call me Lilly. Sometimes I prefer Lilly."

"No, I'm sorry," Emma hesitated and then continued. "I'm afraid there is a misunderstanding, Lilly. We mean the artist, the old woman. The one who walks with a walker and breathes bottled oxygen."

"Oh, her. You mean Granny Blue. Did she tell you she lived in a shoe?"

"What? No."

"Did she tell you she was me?"

"Not exactly," Emma answered. "I just assumed. Not that she was you, but that she was the artist—the real artist."

"Don't I look real? I don't think you should make assumptions. Granny Blue didn't paint that painting—I did. Assumptions are frequently wrong. At least that's what I've found in my experience."

"Yes, I know, but...."

"Granny Blue has dementia. She's a

wicked thing who is liable to say or do anything."

"So you painted the picture?" Emma asked with incredulity. "The one in the gallery?"

"Yes, I did. It was me—me, myself, and I."

"And you are Lilith?"

"I am."

"But you said to call you Lilly?"

"I know. My name is Lilly Lilith. Sometimes I am Lilith Lilly."

"What? Why would you do that?"

"Why not? It depends on my mood, and the owl said it would be all right. The owl knows everything. He is very wise. But it also depends on what day of the week it is, or if Granny Blue is in her shoe or not. If she's baking gingerbread cookies, well then that would be a determinate. It doesn't depend on anything, I just do it. It helps me cope. It lessons the boredom." She tossed her hair, smiling and giggling and acting like she was very pleased with her answer.

"And today you are Lilly?"

"You got it."

"And tomorrow? Will you be Lilly or Lilith?"

"Who can say? It's possible, even likely, but by no means a certainty. I could be the Queen of Sheba, tomorrow. Do you think a cow can really jump over the moon?"

"What?"

"In the nursery rhyme. *Hey diddle diddle the cat and the fiddle, the cow jumped over the moon....* Did he do it? I mean, really?"

"I couldn't say. It's a nursery rhyme. It was written for children." Emma paused and glanced at Ryan. Then she turned back to Lilly. "I'm sorry, I find it a little difficult to believe that you painted those pictures. I mean... no disrespect intended, but you're little more than a child. You couldn't be more than twenty years old. I have a daughter older than you."

"Oh, I am older than I look. It's all very mysterious."

"Well, how old are you?"

"I'll never tell." She giggled like a little girl.

"And you're telling me," Emma said, "that you are really the artist?"

"That's right."

"Whoever painted that picture is extremely talented. The person would have to be classically trained, or have years of experience—maybe a lifetime, a long lifetime. I don't think you would qualify."

"Thank you for the compliment. I accept. But still, I can see you don't believe me. Would you like me to prove it?"

"How can you do that?"

"I can tell you about the owl."

"The owl?"

"Yes, you see:

A wise old owl lived in an oak;
The more he saw the less he spoke;
The less he spoke the more he heard:
Why can't we all be like that bird?"

"Very cute, but how does that prove anything?"

"I'm not sure it does, but I like it. Maybe I could draw your picture. I can make a sketch using charcoal or chalk. It would only take a few minutes. Sketches are simple. You'd be easy to catch."

"How much would it cost us?"

"Don't be silly. I don't charge money for sketching. It would be my pleasure. I love to draw."

"Really?"

"Yes, of course. You sit in that chair yonder, and I will get my chalk."

Emma walked to the chair by the easel and sat down. Ryan accompanied her and stood behind the chair.

"She seems a little nuts," Emma whispered. "She's talking like a hillbilly."

"Maybe she's from the south."

"Nobody talks like that any more."

In a few moments, Lilly emerged with her chalk.

It didn't take long. In what appeared to be breathtaking speed, the girl stopped drawing and said, "Okay, come and have a look-see."

Emma and Ryan stood and walked over to the easel. They couldn't believe their eyes. The picture of Emma was an incredible likeness. It was astonishing.

"My God," Ryan said. "You captured the essence of her completely. That is exactly Emma. I've never seen anything like it."

"Aw shucks... 'taint nothing." The girl held out the drawing to Emma. "Take it, girl."

Emma accepted the offering as if it were a prize of great wealth. "Thank you," she managed to mutter. "I don't know what to say. I'm overwhelmed."

"You're welcome. Now, if I have convinced you that I am who I say I am, what about that painting? What would you like to talk about?"

"Well, my first question is about the perspective. It was from a dog's or wolf's perspective. Am I right?"

Lilly growled, doing an imitation of a wolf. "Yes," she said, "the big, bad wolf."

"Was I the jogger?"

"What? Of course not. I didn't know you, silly. The whole scene was something I imagined."

"And you also painted *The Tree of Hope*, the one with the babies sprouting out of the tree?"

"Yes, I did. I'm quite proud of that one. I won't sell it. If that's what you're going to ask...."

"No, of course not. I wouldn't sell it either. It is an extraordinary picture—so imaginative."

Ryan said, "Did I tell you I am a professor?"

"Yes, doctor, I believe you did. I am very

glad to make your acquaintance."

While Ryan and Lilly chatted together, Emma thought about the picture and then it came to her why it looked different the second time she saw it. There were vines hanging from the branches and wrapped around the trunk. Emma was sure the first time she observed the tree there were no vines. Then Emma remembered a childhood rhyme:

Leaves of three...
Let it be.

Poison ivy, or maybe poison oak. That's what was hanging from *The Tree of Hope*.

"Excuse me," Emma said. "Was there poison ivy on the tree, the one in the picture?"

"I don't know. I was just painting a scene I saw someplace. Either I was painting from nature or it was something I dreamed up in my head. There weren't any monkeys. I first painted the tree and then later I added the babies budding from the trunk and branches. I did that part in my studio. Do you like the picture? Do you think I should have painted monkeys?"

"No, not really. I mean I like the picture,

but I don't think monkeys would have added to it. My question is whether or not the tree had vines hanging from it, or did you first paint the tree without vines?"

"Why would I paint vines if I didn't paint monkeys? It doesn't make sense. Who would swing on the vines? Not the babies. Babies don't swing from vines. If I had added a few monkeys, that would have made sense. That would have been different. I could have named the piece *Monkey Business*, instead of *The Tree of Hope*. What do you think?"

"No, I don't think so."

"But *Monkey Business* could be a metaphor for life. It would be a profound statement on the condition of the world, and man's place within it. I could have even had a banana lying on the ground. Bananas are funny. What do you think?"

"Too much. It would be taking a beautiful painting and making it ridiculous, like a cartoon. The painting is perfect as it is. And a banana on the ground is silly. People wouldn't get the joke. Besides, the painting is already done. All I'm asking is if you first painted the picture with or without vines."

Lilly raised her voice like a petulant

child, "I don't remember." She placed her hands on her head and opened her eyes wide and contorted her face. "How many times do I have to say it; I painted that picture a long time ago."

Emma remained unmoved by Lilly's outburst, "But it couldn't have been that long ago. I mean, considering your age."

"You'd be surprised. It was a long time ago. Things were different then. I was different." She lowered her voice and changed her tone back to normal speech. Then she backed away, looking at Emma suspiciously. She began to move back and forth.

Emma thought, *She is sizing us up like a predator might size up prey. She's deciding how to proceed, what to do with us.* Suddenly Lilly stopped moving and smiled. She tossed her hair and laughed a little-girl laugh. *"The owl and the pussycat went to sea in a beautiful pea green boat....* Have you heard that one? I can recite it from memory." She seemed so enthusiastic, like a small child.

"Yes, Lilly, I heard that poem when I was a little girl. Thank you for answering my question about the painting. I'm afraid we have to leave now. Ryan needs to get back to work."

"So soon?" She hung her head and started to pout. "I thought you might share my mushrooms. We could break bread together."

"I'm sorry, we don't have time."

"Look, about those vines...." Her voice became more serious, adult-like, "I'm a painter. That's what I do. Sometimes I paint the same picture a dozen times. It's how I practice, how I develop technique. If I'm painting a bowl of fruit, I usually paint it several times. Each painting will be little different. Some paintings might have an apple, others an orange. There is no rhyme or reason as to why. So when I painted *The Tree of Hope*, some versions probably had vines, and some didn't. What difference does it make? Who cares? It's just a picture."

"I see. I understand now. Thank you for your time, Lilly. I'm afraid we really must go. We're on a tight schedule."

"If you return, I'll recite *The Owl and the Pussycat* for you. I'm very dramatic."

"I'm sure that would be interesting. I look forward to it."

"Okay then. I've enjoyed talking. I hope you'll come again."

"It's a beautiful day—a good day to paint."

Lilly looked around. "Yes, Emma, you are right. The lighting is perfect. I think I will paint today."

6

The semester went fast. Ryan noticed the older he got, the faster the semesters seemed to go. Now it was summer. He felt fortunate that the university was offering two courses that he was assigned to teach. This was above his normal teaching load. Ryan looked forward to the extra income he would earn for teaching them. The courses were in addition to his usual summer assignment of supervising field-training students. Field-training was experiential-learning that students engaged in upon completion of their coursework. It was their last assignment in order to fulfill the requirements for graduation.

On this morning in early July, there was a knock on Ryan's office door. It was so soft it was barely audible.

"Is someone there?"

The door slowly opened. A student hesitantly inched into the small office and closed the door behind her.

"No, please leave the door open," Dr. Dennison said.

The student opened the door again and

then turned back around. "I'm Jill," she said, "Jill Peterson. I have an appointment."

Ryan observed the student, who was of normal height and weight with stringy dirty-blond hair. She was not unattractive, but her hair needed to be washed and she had a disheveled appearance. Ryan noticed she wore pajama bottoms and rubber flip-flops. It never ceased to amaze him that a student would come to school wearing pajamas. *The world is changing,* he thought. *At least she's not covered in tattoos.* The student looked like she had been crying. Her eyes were red and puffy.

"I was fired," she whimpered. Her voice was soft and Ryan had trouble hearing her.

"I'm sorry, I didn't hear you clearly. What did you say?"

"Dr. Dennison," the girl said, "I was fired. They asked me to leave and not return."

"I don't understand. Who fired you?"

"Father Phil."

Hearing the name of the priest who ran the drug rehabilitation program enabled Ryan to connect the dots. "Are you telling me you were asked to leave your field-training assignment?"

"Yes." She began to sob and rub her eyes with the back of her hands.

"Wait," Ryan said, "you can't be fired from a field-training. You're not even earning a salary. You're paying them for the privilege of learning. You're working for free. I've never heard of a student being fired from an internship. How long have you been there? It hasn't even been one semester, has it?"

"Three weeks. I was in the middle of my fourth week."

"What happened? You must have done something wrong."

"No, I didn't." The tears continued to flow. "I did everything right. I was the first person to arrive in the morning and the last one to leave. I worked hard, Dr. Dennison. I really did."

"Who asked you to leave?"

"Father Phil." The girl was crying.

"And you say you didn't do anything wrong? You didn't make any mistakes? Did you do something that you weren't supposed to do? Did you fail to do something?"

"No, sir—nothing like that."

"What did Father Phil say to you? Tell

me the exact words."

"He said I didn't need to come back; they wouldn't be needing my services any longer. I told him I wanted to return, but he said no. He was very specific, I'm not to come back."

"And that was all? Did he give you an explanation why he didn't want you to finish?"

"No. That was all he said."

Ryan wrote some notes on a pad of paper. Then he tore out the page, went to the file cabinet and removed a file.

"Jill Peterson. Is that right? Is that who you are?"

"Yes."

"And you were doing a six-week field placement at the Phoenix Recovery Center?"

"Yes, sir."

"Look, Jill, I am going to need a little time to investigate this situation. Can you come back after the weekend? Why don't we set an appointment for the same time on Monday. Would that be all right?"

"Yes, Dr. Dennison. I will see you then." She turned and left the office, shuffling her flip-flops against the vinyl floor.

Ryan wrote a note to himself on his pad.

He headed the page, *Things to Do* and then beneath the heading wrote *see Father Phil at Phoenix*. Typically he didn't like visiting the drug program because he had found in the past that Father Phil was an authoritarian and opinionated individual. He was not an easy person to work with—not for the student interns and not for him as their adviser. But Ryan was glad to have something to do after his office hours were finished. Maybe by keeping busy he could get his mind off that girl—Lilly. Ever since he and Emma met the artist, he hadn't been able to stop thinking about her. She was so bright and cheery. It was as if her image had been seared into his flesh. He was more than distracted; he was obsessed. And he couldn't understand it. He couldn't explain why.

As a college professor Ryan was around attractive women all the time. Generally speaking he never gave any of them a second thought. He didn't make unwelcome overtures or suggestive comments. Not any more. Not since *the Heather incident*. For the last decade he had behaved exemplarily.

He didn't imply anything unseemly to students, not even in a humorous manner.

These days, Ryan thought of himself as a consummate professional; a man who always kept his office door open whenever a co-ed came for advice or a student conference. Ryan hoped others would observe him. He wanted witnesses to see all that was happening within his tiny office. He wanted to avoid any appearance of impropriety. That was what being a professional was about. Ryan would not jeopardize all he had accomplished through the years by being stupid now. Not again.

He had seen what happens when professors get involved personally with students. It's fun in the beginning, passion run amok, but it almost always ends badly. How many professors had Ryan observed through the years who lost their careers, marriages, and families by fooling around with students? Ryan could think of three colleagues right off the bat, not counting his own episode. It never worked out. Given enough time, the arrangements always crashed and burned.

More to the point, Ryan loved his wife. He was not a philanderer. He hadn't the least desire to stray, and it had been that way for the last decade. Ryan was a happily married man. He and Emma were not like the couples one occasionally saw in restaurants looking miserable and not communicating with one another. No, that was not his marriage—not any more. Ever since he started going to meetings and got his drinking under control, things improved.

Emma was so patient and understanding. She was his best friend, his lover, and the mother of his children. It would be inconceivable for him to cheat again. He was lucky he hadn't lost his job back then. His marriage was even stronger, perfect—well, almost perfect.

So why am I so preoccupied with this woman, Lilly? I've totally lost all objectivity and I do not like the feeling of being helpless; of being driven by another human being—a stranger. Could I be having a mid-life crisis? After all, I am fifty. Ryan looked at his watch. *Only two more hours and I can leave. Maybe I can go to her house by myself. I know nothing about her. Is she married or single? Does she live by herself or with that daffy old lady? Maybe she's a student. Did I tell her I am a professor? Would she be impressed? I wonder if she likes me? I can use the Phoenix House as an excuse for getting home late. I can tell Emma that I had to see Father Phil about Jill Peterson. The poor girl is so distressed. I am just doing my job.*

It wasn't as if he entirely wanted to go to see Lilly; he didn't. On one level he was repulsed by the thought, and intellectually he knew it was wrong to go. He had no reason to travel in the opposite direction, twelve miles out of the way from his home, but he could not keep himself from going. He wasn't in control; he was floating like a leaf on a stream, and he knew where that stream was headed.

7

When Ryan arrived at the end of the private road he saw Lilly to the side of the cottage in front of her easel with a paint brush in her hand. She was wearing cutoff blue jeans and a white t-shirt, smeared with paint. She was just a wisp of a girl, like a fairy princess. Ryan half expected to see wings and witness Lilly lift off the ground like a dragonfly.

"Hi, Ryan. You're back. Is it all right to call you Ryan, or would you prefer Dr. Dennison?"

"Ryan is fine. I'm surprised you remembered my name at all. I was here only once and that was three months ago."

"I remember. Maybe because you left a big impression."

"I did?"

"You certainly did. You're an impressive man, professor. Is there a particular reason you came today, or did you just want to come out and play?"

"I was wondering if you would show me

more of your artwork. You see, my wife will be having a birthday and I want to get her a present—something unique and special. I thought maybe you had a picture you would be willing to part with."

"When is her birthday?"

"In March, but I like to be prepared."

"That's nine months from now. You didn't see anything in the gallery—in all the galleries—that pleased you?"

"Actually, to be honest, I haven't looked. It was your work I wanted, so I thought I'd come directly to the source."

"How complimentary." She put down her paint brush and smiled. A breeze blew, tossing her hair about and pressing her T-shirt against her body. Her breasts were round and full, and Ryan could see she wasn't wearing a bra. It excited him and he forced himself to keep from staring.

"Would you like some tea?" Lilly inquired.

"That would be lovely," Ryan replied.

She led him to the cottage. Inside it was cozy, with a round oak table and four chairs. One wall was lined with bookshelves from floor to ceiling and was filled with many volumes. It was dark inside. A large stone fireplace stood in the middle of the living room, between the living room and kitchen. Overall, the room left a romantic, other-worldly impression on Ryan.

"Let's light some candles," Lilly said. She lit a few and placed them in various locations.

In the flickering candle light, the room was mysterious. It reminded him of his college days when he had beads hanging in the doorways and psychedelic posters on the wall. Illuminated by a black-light, they glowed in the dark. He was bearded then, with long hair. It was a time in his life when he regarded himself as a rebel and thought he could change the world. Ryan half expected Lilly would emerge holding a bag of marijuana and the two of them could get high together. What was it that Timothy Leary had said? *Turn on, tune in, drop out*, the mantra of the sixties. Ryan always felt he should have been born earlier. In his heart, he was a man of the sixties—a free thinker, a hippy. He would have loved going to Woodstock. Unfortunately he wasn't old enough. He was born a decade too late.

Lilly didn't offer any grass. She went to the stove and put the kettle on to boil.

"It's lovely here," Ryan said, looking around to absorb the surroundings. "It reminds me of my college days. It's very charming." He noticed a few antiques and many paintings stacked against the walls. "You are prolific. You must spend a great deal of your time painting."

"I do. I love to paint. Besides, I don't get many visitors, and I'm bored."

"Is that why you have so many books? You must be a reader. I can't help but notice that some of your books look very old. You don't see many that are leather bound any more. They could be valuable."

She smiled and opened a kitchen drawer and removed a computer tablet. "See?" she said, "I keep up with the times. I'm a modern woman. I do most of my reading these days on my tablet."

"I can't believe you would ever be bored."

"Me? You have trouble believing I find life boring?" Suddenly, the expression on her face changed. "I'm surprised that you're surprised. Actually, that is really not the best way to say it. Life isn't merely boring, it's fucking boring!" She raised the volume of her voice for emphasis. "Write those words down in boldface, and then underscore the text. Listen to me. Life is fucking boring!"

Ryan was stunned. Not so much by the language, which was a surprise in and of itself, but by the vitriol with which Lilly expressed her feelings. Her whole countenance changed. She switched from an innocent, naïve, child-like figure to a snarling beast. She looked hard, disillusioned, and incredibly mean. She reminded Ryan of a cobra rising up to strike. Ryan felt the need to do something quickly to defuse the situation.

"Will you show me some of your work?" He said it softly, almost apologetically. "Are any paintings for sale?"

Her appearance suddenly reverted to her former self. "Yes, Ryan," she said sweetly, "I will be glad to show you. But if you want to buy a painting, why don't you just go and see old Metcalf? Or, you could go to one of the other galleries. You don't have to buy my painting."

"But I want to. That's the point. I only want one of yours, Lilly."

"Thank you, you're a sweetheart."

"Where's the old lady, the person you referred to as Granny Blue?"

"That old creature? I can't say, because I don't know. She could be anywhere, flittering about, causing mischief, or making trouble for someone, somewhere."

"Is she related to you? Is she your grandmother, or aunt, or some kind of kin?"

"Something like that. Try my tea and see if you like it. It's my own recipe." She placed a cup before him and filled it.

"It's not regular, store-bought tea?"

"Yes, and no. I start with ordinary pekoe tea leaves and add some spices and herbs that I grow in my garden. Then I sprinkle it with my magic and....whoosh: Lilly's Wonder Elixir. The cure for what ails you. I call it my anti-melancholy/have-a-nice-day brew."

"But I'm not melancholy, I'm perfectly fine."

"Good. I'm glad to hear that. Then the tea will enhance your well-being. It will make your good day even better." She walked to the wall and picked up a pile of paintings and placed them on the table. "Go through these. See if any appeal to you. Tell me. Be honest. I have enough faith in my work that

I can take constructive criticism."

Ryan began to scan through the paintings. Most were pictures of nature scenes, two were of floral arrangements, and one was fruit in a bowl. "I can't believe you painted these. I mean they're so... professional. Beautiful. I can't criticize anything about your work. It's perfect. Your paintings belong in a museum, not on a kitchen table. They have that quality about them. All I can do is offer praise."

"Thank you. You're very kind, and a wonderful art critic, if I do say so myself."

Ryan was starting to feel sleepy. He was thinking that Lilly seemed different than when he met her in April. She wasn't speaking in riddles, nor was she giggling and acting like a child or lunatic. She looked quite grown-up, and overtly sexual. "Lilly, I have to ask. Are you married?"

"No, Ryan, I'm not married." Her voice was soft and low-pitched. "Should I be? You're embarrassing me. Would you feel better if I were?"

"No... but I was wondering about your age. How old you are. Can I ask?"

"You can ask, but I won't tell you. Not the truth. I would make up a number. I would tell you what I think you want to hear. Women don't like to tell their age, Ryan. Don't you know that?"

"Why not?"

"Because...."

She was saying something, but he couldn't make out the rest of her answer. The words were jumbled. They blurred together and Ryan couldn't distinguish one word from the next. As he looked to Lilly for an explanation all he saw was her face— distorted and stretched as if he was looking at her in a carnival mirror. She was smiling and he heard strange noises in the background. Colors seemed muted. From a purple-green fog Ryan thought, she is so beautiful, so angelic... so very perfect. The last thing he heard was "Rest.... You'll feel better."

And he did. When he awoke he felt like a million dollars.

"Did you drug me?" he asked.

"Don't be silly. You fell asleep. I bet you already had a hard day at work before you came here. You were tired. And the tea is soothing, isn't it? It's a special blend, but just tea—nothing more. It just relaxed you. Do you feel better now?"

"I do. I feel terrific. I can't remember when I last felt so rested." Ryan looked at his watch. "I'd better go home. My wife will be worried. May I come back again? I would love to continue our visit. You are a very interesting person."

"Of course, you are welcome, any time. Don't be a stranger."

Ryan left Lilly's company, got in his car and headed home. He was late and he was worried. What would he tell Emma? He was sure she would be upset. What he didn't know was how upset, and he was a little afraid to find out. But he felt so damn good. He felt like he could conquer the world. And that girl, Lilly, she was so refreshing, so incredibly terrific. He needed a drink— *Something to even me out before I face the old battle axe.*

When he came to the Wagon Wheel Tavern, he turned his car into the parking lot.

Jim Pahz

8

"You're late. I was beginning to worry."

"I'm sorry, Emma. I had things to do at school." He embraced his wife and kissed her.

"What kind of things?" Emma asked.

"Student things, with internships."

"What do you mean?"

"Just that some are not working out so well. I have a few problems."

Emma hesitated and looked at Ryan critically. Then she stepped back from him and asked, "Ryan, have you been drinking?"

"No, of course not." Ryan turned and began to walk away.

Emma followed. "I can smell it on your breath."

"Well... maybe just one or two."

"Oh no." She put her hands to her forehead expressing alarm. "You know better than that. When was the last time you attended a meeting?"

"Emma, don't start. I'm a grown man. I can take care of myself."

"No, Ryan, you can't. You're an alcoholic. Did you forget? Isn't the first step, 'we admitted to ourselves we were powerless over alcohol'? You once had the courage to admit that. Ryan, you almost lost your job. Don't you remember how much trouble you got into with your department? You were denied promotion. Remember your humiliation in front of the promotion committee? Remember Heather? Ryan, you're so close. I'm sure when you go up for promotion again you will get it. They can't keep you at the bottom level forever. Please don't screw it up—not again."

"That was ten years ago. And I haven't had a drink since then."

"You mean, not until today."

"It's not a big deal."

"Yes, Ryan, it is a big deal—a very big deal."

"Okay, Emma, I'm sorry. I apologize. I won't do it again."

"Ryan, I want you to go to a meeting. They're important. I'll go with you. If you can find an open meeting, we can go together. Or you can go alone, whichever you prefer. But go. That's the important thing. Something's going on with you. I'm not sure what it is, but that's not what's important. Whatever it is, the meetings are the best place for you to be. They're like the rudder on a sail boat. They make it possible for you to steer your boat and go in the right direction. Otherwise, you get blown off course and drift wherever the wind takes you. That's not good, Ryan."

"Okay, Emma. I'll go. If that's what you want. Now please... enough with the whining. Stop nagging me."

"It's not what I want, Ryan, it's what you need. Ryan, you promise? When will you begin?"

"I'll look into it. It's been a long time and I'll have to investigate where the meetings are being held. I'll find out tomorrow and then I'll start. I promise."

***

10:00 a.m., Monday morning. Ms. Jill Peterson was back and stood facing her professor. She wasn't wearing pajamas and flip-flops, and apparently made an effort to improve her appearance. She was appropriately attired and her hair no longer looked dirty and greasy. Cleaned up she was a surprisingly good-looking girl. Ryan was impressed. "Good morning Jill. I met with Father Phil last Friday regarding your placement, and I think we have a few things to talk about."

"What did he say?"

"He said that you are no longer living in the dormitory, but have moved into an apartment with a client. Is that true?"

"Well, technically, but …."

"Jill, there is no technicality involved. You're not a politician. The answer is either yes or no."

"Well then, I suppose I would have to say yes."

"I see. And this person you are living with is an individual you were counseling as part of your duties at the Phoenix Center?"

"Yes."

"Jill, were you aware that this man is married and that he has two young children?"

"Yes, Dr. Dennison, I knew that."

"And nevertheless, knowing this, you became involved with him?"

"Yes."

"And you see nothing wrong with your

behavior?"

"It's personal. It is out of the purview of my work or school assignments. It is strictly between me and Billy. In other words, it's a private matter."

"Jill, he was your client. You were his counselor. You violated just about every rule of the counseling profession. What about professional ethics, or a code of conduct? Don't these things mean anything to you?"

"Yes, Dr. Dennison. I remember those concepts from class. But Billy and I have something special, something more important."

"And what is that?"

"Love. We fell in love. To my way of thinking, love trumps everything else. Besides, when all is said and done, Dr. Dennison, those concepts are just words." She spoke defiantly, not like the weepy girl who stood before him last week. Today she was standing her ground and would not be moved.

"Well, Jill, I can't help you. Your internship is terminated. It's over."

"Can I get a refund?"

"No, I'm sorry, you can't. You failed

the assignment. It's the same as failing an academic course."

"Dr. Dennison, you're my advisor. Can't you help me? My parents are not wealthy people. It's hard on them to pay for my university studies. My dad has two jobs and I don't want to disappoint them. It would break their hearts." She began to cry.

Ryan hesitated, turning the matter over in his head. He felt conflicted. He could never deal with a crying woman. It was one of his weaknesses. Finally he said, "Look, Jill, here is what I can do for you. I can assign a grade of I, an incomplete, for your field-training experience. I will try to find another placement for you, but it will have to be in fall semester."

"Fall semester! But I was expecting to graduate at the end of summer."

"I'm sorry. Summer is half over. Normally, summer is the only time of the academic year that internships are done. In your case, we're going to have to do something different. I will need to get special permission from the department to allow you to repeat your field-training experience in the fall."

"But that means I won't be able to

graduate on time."

"Yes, Jill, it does. You will have to remain one more semester here at this university, but at least you will be permitted to graduate. Of course, that is contingent on a successful completion of your assignment."

"Will I have to pay another tuition?"

"No, not with the grade of incomplete assigned. I won't say anything about your efforts at Phoenix House. If asked, I will say you got sick and were unable to finish. If you can complete the second placement, without incident, then I will remove your incomplete grade and assign you a final grade. There is only one of two grades you can receive— pass or fail."

"Thank you, Dr. Dennison. You're so kind and understanding. When can I expect to start?"

"Not until fall semester. Come back and see me at the beginning of the semester. Until then, enjoy the remainder of your summer. In the fall, I will let you know where to go and with whom to speak."

"What type of program will it be? Will it be another counseling position?"

"No, Jill. It will be something completely

different. Probably it will be some type of work in the health department, or maybe I can get you something in an elementary school. You shouldn't have been counseling in the first place. You were never trained to be a counselor—not really. Besides, you're not licensed. You had a couple of courses, but that doesn't qualify you to work with individuals in a one-on-one situation. Why were you doing that anyway?"

"They were short on staff. Father Phil said his budget had been cut. I was only counseling court referrals. Most people didn't want to be there to begin with. They had to come or they would be put in jail. It was a captive audience."

"And that's where you met your boyfriend, this Billy person?"

"Yes. I think it was love at first sight. I believe in such things. Don't you, Dr. Dennison?"

"That's a romantic concept, but you were not on equal terms with Billy. You were his therapist. You had a position of authority. You should never let personal feelings interfere with your work. If you get such feelings you are supposed to withdraw. Your client can be assigned to another counselor. Later, after Billy has completed his course of treatment, and, if you subsequently meet him socially, that might be a different matter."

"I know, I should have waited. I couldn't help myself."

"Well, if you know it, it seems to me that you acted selfishly. You were only thinking of yourself."

"I suppose."

"All right, Jill, I am not going to sermonize to you. That's not my job. You will have to live with the consequence of your behavior. In my professional opinion, what you did was wrong, very wrong, and you should have known better. Honestly, I don't really believe you deserve a second chance. Your field-training is supposed to be your capstone experience. It's the culmination of your education. But it's over now. On a personal level, I hope this relationship with Billy works out for the both of you and you live happily ever after. I have my doubts."

"He's filing for a divorce."

"Of course he is. Jill, what can I say? Check back with us in the fall. Meanwhile, I will try to locate another placement."

Jim Pahz

9

"Hello, everyone. My name is Alfred and I'm an alcoholic."

In unison, the group responded, "Hello Alfred."

The speaker was an old-timer. He was an elderly man who looked to be in his 70s or 80s. Like the other participants at the meeting of Alcoholics Anonymous, Ryan sat respectfully waiting for the man to say his piece. He didn't want to be there. He only came because of Emma. He wanted to have something good to tell her. Maybe then she would get off his back and stop nagging.

"I've been drinking most of my life," the speaker began. "There was a time when I had a family, a good career, and all the trappings of a successful life. Not any more. Not in a very long time. I can say without hesitation that I lost it all to drinking. Alcohol stole my life from me. No, that's not really true. I gave it away, willingly. Nobody put a gun to my head. Nobody made me drink.

"I remember once, after I had lost my

job and family, I was living by myself in the Towers on Livingston Street. It was subsidized housing and it was in the 1970s. At that time you could only buy your booze from a state-licensed liquor store. The liquor stores all closed at midnight. So one night I go for my bottle and I see it's empty. I look all around the apartment, check my usual hiding places—the cupboard, beneath the couch, in the water tank behind the toilet—nothing." A muffled sound of laughter filled the room.

"No booze, anywhere. I panicked. I look at my watch." The speaker lifted his arm and went through the motions of checking his watch. "And I see it's 11:45 p.m. I got fifteen minutes before the liquor store closes.

"Now at this time, I'm not dressed. I'm in my pajamas and I'm on the fifth floor of the Marcus Towers on Livingston Street. There is a liquor store across the street on the corner, at the intersection of Livingston and Main Street. So I put on my bathrobe and slippers and I get to the lobby in no time flat and race outside, heading to the liquor store. The only problem was, it was a night in January and we had just had about a foot of fresh snow that afternoon.

"I'm running down the block, through the snow, in my bare feet and slippers, oblivious to the inclement weather. My only concern is to get to the liquor store on time, before it closes. And fortunately, I do. I arrive five minutes before midnight. Lucky me! So I buy two bottles of Jack Daniels and put one in each pocket of my bathrobe. I start hoofing it back to the Towers, when I suddenly become aware—hey, it's cold outside. My feet are getting numb. I'm turning blue. I'm freezing.

"So I'm moving faster and faster—to get home and to get in from the cold. And just when I'm approaching the Towers, and think I'm home free, I step on a patch of ice and my legs slip out from under me and I fall backwards. So now I'm covered in snow. I lay there for a few minutes, trying to get my bearings. Then I get to my feet and I feel liquid running down the back of my legs. My booze! But before I reach into my pockets to check my bottles, I begin to pray. I pray—*please God, let it be blood!*"

There is another muffled sound of laughter as people reflect on the comic elements of the story, and on the entirety of the tragedy.

"When I looked behind me, in the direction I had just come from, I saw the lights illuminating the liquor store had been turned off. The store was closed. My bottles were broken. My booze was gone, and I was wet and cold. I was so fucking cold."

Another chuckle from the crowd.

I've got to get out of here, Ryan thought. *I don't need this. I better go home.*

10

"You told her what?"

Ryan looked sheepish. He dropped his head and looked at the floor as he told his story about Jill Peterson.

Emma looked at him with disgust. "You gave her another chance? He was a married man, for goodness sake, with children. What's wrong with you? What were you thinking? You should have told her she failed her assignment and that was the end of it. She could pay her tuition the following semester and try again. That would have been more than fair. No degree. She doesn't deserve to represent your department or university."

"I know, but I...."

"You what? Are you going to tell me what a nice guy you are? Jesus Christ, Ryan, what's wrong with you?" Emma paused and looked at her husband, re-evaluating his character and behavior. "I bet she was pretty. Wasn't she? She was a good-looking student with a pretty face and a nice body, and you couldn't help yourself. It sounds like Heather all over again. You didn't go sunbathing together again. Not this time, I hope."

"She said it would break her parents' hearts if she failed. She said her daddy had two jobs."

"Oh, the poor dear! What could you do? Ryan, don't you see how she played you? She gave you a sob story and you bought it—hook, line, and sinker. You just believed everything this girl told you because you wanted to believe it. It's your kind of a drama. That's just who you are. You're so kind and compassionate, but just a little pathetic."

"I'm sorry."

"Don't apologize to me. You don't owe me anything. Apologize to yourself. Your behavior reflects on your character, or your lack of character. It shows the stuff you're made of. If you want to apologize, then apologize to your department. Hell, apologize to the university.

"You're a sweet man, Ryan, but you're weak. You're a push-over. You lack character and you always take the easy way out—the path of least resistance. I don't know what makes you this way; it's just who you are. But by behaving in this manner you put your job in jeopardy...and your family too. Isn't the policy of the university, as stated in the catalogue, that an instructor issues a grade of incomplete only if the student is doing passing work but needs to discontinue because of some type of emergency? I believe it says that. Your student didn't have an emergency; she *was* the emergency. It was all her fault. And you're wishing her well? You're telling her it's all right; you will help her get a second chance? My God! You're the prince on the white horse ready to ride in and rescue her? And you believe all the crap about her poor parents and her daddy's two jobs? Give me a break.

"I'm disappointed in you, Ryan. You should know better. There is absolutely no way that sleeping with your client can be interpreted as doing passing work. But maybe you failed to cover that topic in class. And, I know you're drinking again. Don't deny it." Emma turned and walked out of the room. She went to their bedroom and slammed the door behind her.

Ryan felt bad. He was ashamed of himself. Deep down, Ryan knew that Emma was correct. She was a little harsh in her condemnation, but she was right. Why did he behave as he did with that student? He didn't know the answer. Was it because she was a good-looking girl, or because he was weak? Maybe it was for both reasons. He didn't like confrontation and would avoid one whenever he could. Besides, he could never resist a crying woman. His daughters learned that lesson a long time ago and always used it to their advantage. If it hadn't been for Emma, those kids would have grown up to be monsters. Emma was always the disciplinarian. Ryan was putty in their hands, a push-over. Yes, Emma was right. He was a weak man. He knew this about himself and because of his weakness, he hated himself.

11

Throughout the fall semester, Ryan managed to stay away from Lilly. It wasn't easy, and it took a lot of willpower. He found he was completely preoccupied with her, wondering throughout the day how she spent her time, and what she could be doing at any given hour. *Why,* Ryan wondered, *did Lilly seem so silly on that first visit, but so mature and adult-like on the second visit? She was almost sultry.* It didn't make sense. But he finally concluded it was because she was an artist. *Artists are sensitive and finely-tuned like a well-bred race horse. So Lilly is temperamental and a bit eccentric. That could only be expected.*

At school, Ryan had difficulty concentrating. He didn't want to be there. During departmental meetings, his mind wandered. He sat at the table doodling on his writing pad. If asked a question, he would find it necessary to have the question repeated. His work suffered, and he was ineffective in the classroom. Even the students remarked on his absent-mindedness. They made jokes about him. One student went so far as to lodge a complaint with Ryan's department chairperson. And all of this was because of Lilly. He simply couldn't get his mind off that remarkable girl. She must be one in a million.

***

By November, the weather had turned cold again and it was snowing. One morning while the Dennisons were sitting at the breakfast table, their conversation was interrupted by a gunshot. The sound was so loud and seemed so close to the house, it alarmed both Ryan and Emma.

"What was that?" Emma asked.

"I'd better have a look." Ryan said as he went to the closet and grabbed a fleece-lined parka.

Outside, Ryan looked around trying to determine where the shot had come from. About fifty feet from the garden, which was just to the left of the house, a man dressed in orange stood facing the garden, which was enclosed with a white aluminum fence. It had been an expensive proposition to install the fence, more than five thousand dollars, but it was the only way to keep out the deer and Emma had wanted a deer-proof garden. But now, as Ryan faced the enclosure, he saw that a large buck was standing inside at the rear of the garden, facing the man in orange who had his gun raised and pointed at the animal.

"Hold on," Ryan yelled at the man. "You're on private property. You can't shoot that animal here."

"That's my deer," the man responded.

"I don't care whose deer it is. You're trespassing. You can't just come on a person's land and discharge a firearm. What's wrong with you?"

"The law says I can come on your property if I'm in pursuit of my quarry."

"Not without permission. And you don't have my permission."

"When I began this morning I was on State land. The animal ran here and I followed. It jumped the fence."

"That fence is seven feet high. The garden was designed to keep the deer out."

"It jumped it, I tell you. It sailed right

over it like it wasn't even there."

"Be that as it may, it's now standing in my wife's garden and, as far as I'm concerned, that's a sanctuary. You don't have my permission. If you take another shot I will call the police and have you arrested. We are not hunters and my property is a place of tranquility. We love animals and you are disturbing the harmony of our homestead. I won't have it. Trespassing is a serious offense and the penalties are severe."

"I'll tell you what I'm going to do. I'm fixin' to call the DNR, the Department of Natural Resources. It's against the law to keep a wild deer in captivity. We'll see who gets fined."

"Look, mister, you said yourself, the deer jumped the fence. I'm not keeping a wild deer. In fact, I'll open the gate and the deer can run off. But you're still on private property and I don't want anyone shooting a gun so close to my house. My wife is inside. So I suggest you leave. No, 'suggest' is not the right word, I demand you leave."

Ryan walked to the fence and examined it. He saw where the bullet had hit the aluminum. A piece of the piping was cut almost in half. "Jesus Christ," Ryan said, "You're not such a good shot. I hope you have insurance."

He paused for a moment to reflect, then he said, "Look, we have eighty acres. The adjacent land to the west is State land. I presume you came from that direction. That is where you are supposed to hunt and it consists of hundreds of acres. The boundary lines are clearly marked. All those trees that have a white ring around the trunk mark our boundary. If the deer leaves after I open the gate and goes back onto State land, then you're free to pursue it. It will, as you say, be your deer. But right now, he's nobody's deer. Do you understand? I'm prepared to forget that you damaged my fence and let the matter drop. But you have to leave now and no more hunting on my property. Okay?"

"I guess," the man grumbled. "I should have hit that deer. I'm a good shot. If it hadn't been for that girl…. She distracted me."

"Girl?" Ryan looked around, but didn't see anyone. "What girl?"

"Over there." The man pointed to a line of trees about 200 yards away. "She wasn't wearing a coat. I thought it was strange because it is so cold today. I took my eye off the deer for just a minute."

Ryan looked at the man in disbelief. "You saw a girl in the woods, in the snow, and she wasn't wearing a coat?"

"I don't think she had a coat on. It happened rather quickly."

"Look buddy, maybe you're off your meds or something. I don't know, but I seriously doubt anyone's out there romping around in November without a coat. But if you're convinced, then I can call the police. I can get them out here in ten minutes and you can file a report. They can organize a search party or something. It's your call. You tell me what you want me to do."

The man hesitated. He looked in the direction of the tree line. Then he answered, "No, maybe I just thought I saw someone. I could have made a mistake. It might have been smoke. My mind must have been playing tricks on me." He looked around again, searching for the girl. "I guess I was seeing things." Then he began to walk away in the direction of the State land.

"What a jerk," Ryan mumbled under his breath. "Smoke?" Ryan looked at the fence damage more closely. "What's this going to cost me?" he asked himself. "I hope my home owner's policy will cover it." He went back to the house and opened the storm door. A violent blast of wind took the door and slammed it against the side of the house. It took a lot of muscle for Ryan to get it closed again. He entered his house and called, "Emma, you had better come and take a look at this."

Emma got her coat and the two went back outside. Ryan led her to the garden. Inside the buck stood facing them. The animal was breathing hard and steam escaped from flared nostrils.

"How did he get in there?" Emma asked.

"According to the hunter, he jumped."

"No! That fence is seven feet high. It's supposed to be deer-proof."

"I know, but I guess nobody told that to the deer."

"His antlers have nine points; five on one side and four on the other."

"He might have injured himself sometime in the past. That could cause the antlers to be atypical like that, I think."

"What should we do?"

"Unless you want a pet deer, we should open the gate and set it free."

"Yes, that sounds like a good idea. I don't need another pet."

Ryan walked to the gate and opened it. He placed a big rock in front so the wind wouldn't blow the gate closed again. "Go on, fellow. You're free. Have a good life."

The buck just stood there watching them.

"He doesn't seem to want to go," Emma said.

"Let's go back to the house. He'll leave when he's ready. He might still be worried about that idiot hunter."

"What idiot hunter? Do you mean the man who fired the gun?"

"Yes, the man who shot our fence."

"What's a person doing hunting on a day like this? I know it's deer season, but didn't he notice how windy and cold it is? And why did he shoot so close to our house?"

"I said he was an idiot. I suspect he might have been drinking. He told me he saw a girl walking through the snow and she wasn't wearing a coat."

"Really? Did you see a girl?"

"No, of course not. I'm pretty sure there

was no girl, but if there was, she was probably sitting on top of a pink elephant. In that case, she wouldn't need a coat. If there had been a girl, I think that fool would have shot her."

The two walked back and entered their home. About an hour later, a man from the DNR arrived. The ranger introduced himself as Officer Silver. "We received a complaint that you have confined a deer here." The ranger continued, "I must advise you that it is illegal to keep a wild animal in confinement without a permit."

Ryan led the ranger to the garden and showed him the gate that was open. The animal was nowhere to be seen. "We never confined a deer," Ryan said. "One jumped in here earlier this morning. We opened the gate and let it go. As you can see there aren't any animals here."

"I see," the ranger said. "You didn't raise a fawn and keep it?"

"No, of course not. It was a full-grown buck and it jumped the fence. I let it go, just like I said. I have a pretty good idea who lodged the complaint. Some idiot hunter chased the deer from State land. I think he was two sheets to the wind, if you get my drift. He crossed our boundary line which is clearly marked on the trees, and started shooting towards my house."

"Are you saying that he was intoxicated?"

"I believe so. I can't be certain. I didn't give him a breathalyzer or make him walk a line. I can sympathize. It's been really cold. I've been known to pop-a-cork on occasion myself, when the wife isn't looking." Ryan smiled, pleased with himself for his candor.

"He shouldn't be outside with a firearm if he's been drinking. And he never should be shooting so close to your home."

"Absolutely, Officer, that's what I tried to tell him. Let me show you what he did to my fence. Maybe you could give me a copy of the incident report and I can turn a claim in to my insurance company. Then I can get the fence repaired."

"Hard to believe a deer could jump that high," the ranger said.

"Yes, that's what my wife and I thought."

The ranger wrote something down in a notepad and then thanked Ryan and apologized for the inconvenience. "I'll have a copy of the report sent to you."

"Thank you, I appreciate it."

***

Later, around noon, Emma went outside to feed her birds. She had enclosed them in a shed for the winter. The ducks and peafowl were housed in one compartment, the chickens and guinea hens were kept together in another. After finishing her chores, she walked past the house to the garden. She didn't know why she went there; it was still windy but the sun was higher and stronger in the sky. The gate was still open and, as she walked inside, she was aware of a ringing in her ears. *Tinnitus* she thought, *I'm getting old. I'd better see a doctor.*

She had started to close the gate when she noticed next to the house in the corner was the buck. It was so well camouflaged that Emma almost missed seeing him. The deer looked directly at her without moving. Emma smiled, walked through the gate and approached the animal. The two made eye contact.

"Well hi," she said. "So you're back. Did you walk through the gate this time, or did you jump the fence again? You know you're

not supposed to be able to jump that fence.
We had it especially made to keep you and
your buddies out. You might think about
trying out for the deer-Olympics. And you
better be careful if you decide to leave again.
You know it's hunting season and there are a
lot of people lurking about who would love
to shoot you and hang you from a tree. You
have a nice set of antlers—impressive. So
if you want to keep them, I suggest you be
careful."

Then the deer lowered and raised its
head, like it was nodding affirmatively.
"Extraordinary," Emma said out loud. "It's
almost as if you understand me, like you are
agreeing with me."

The deer took two steps towards Emma
and started to paw the ground. Emma froze
and was momentarily frightened. She had
heard stories of people being attacked
by deer. It was rare, but it occasionally
happened. She was about to turn and run, but
then the animal stopped advancing, lowered
and raised its head again, turned and walked
back to the rear corner of the garden.

Emma backed out through the gate,
her heart pounding. She walked backward

towards the house. After about ten steps, she addressed the deer in a loud voice. "In case you decide to stay, I will get you some feed. Would corn work? How about some hay? Yes, yes..., I know I'm not supposed to feed the deer, but it's not like you're just any old deer. You're a high-jumper with a personality who apparently understands English." She turned and walked back to the house. Strange, she thought. Very strange. First the wolf incident, and now this.

That afternoon as they were about to leave for town, she told Ryan about her encounter with the deer.

"Let's see if he's still there."

The two of them put on their coats and walked to the garden. The gate was still open but the garden was empty. Looking at the snow, Emma remarked, "There are no deer prints. The only tracks I see are mine and some bird tracks."

"Turkeys," Ryan responded. "Apparently, after your deer left, a flock of turkeys came in here and covered your deer's tracks with their own."

"It's not my deer," Emma said. "It's a deer, an ordinary deer."

"No, Emma, there's nothing ordinary about that deer. Any animal that behaves oddly, like that one, may be many things— but ordinary is not one of them."

They closed the garden gate.

***

The following morning, Ryan returned to the university. Jill Peterson was engaged in her second field placement assignment. She had been placed at a state facility for the developmentally disabled. Her duty was to supervise a production line consisting of a dozen cognitively challenged individuals who made pot-holders from strands of fabric. It was repetitive and boring work. The workers (clients) were quite happy and appreciated the opportunity to have something useful to do, but Jill was miserable.

When Ryan arrived at his office, Jill was waiting.

"You've got to get me out of there," she said. "It's making me crazy. If I stay much longer I'm going to be retarded."

"Hi, Jill, nice to see you again. You shouldn't call them *retarded*. It's insensitive and unprofessional. It's also not politically correct to use that terminology. Besides you know the reason for your dilemma, but let's go over it again. This is your second assignment. It's your last chance. You can regard it as an opportunity or punishment. Whatever you call it, you're just going to have to force yourself to finish it. You only have a couple of weeks to go and then it will be over. You can't be assigned to another field-placement. Not again. The university won't have it. If you fail to complete this assignment, you will get a grade of F. Then you won't graduate. It's that simple. Think of this challenge like a military obligation. You don't have a choice. You know what people say?"

"No," Jill said, discouraged. "Tell me what they say."

"They say if it doesn't kill you, then it will make you stronger."

"That's good to know, Dr. Dennison. I'm still alive, but I hate this internship. I can't tell you how much I hate it. It is a punishment."

"I'm sorry you feel like that. I'm confident you'll survive. And I hear you're doing a good job. I'm told you are very patient with the workers. It will be over soon, Jill. Hang in there."

***

Jill stuck with it. When the semester was over, she received her passing grade. Her name was put on the graduation list. At the ceremony, as the students proudly marched up to the stage to receive their diplomas, Ryan wondered if Billy was in the audience observing Jill's accomplishment. He wondered if Billy knew the price Jill Peterson paid for their romance.

12

Ryan was drinking again—secretly. He tried to hide it from Emma, but he wasn't successful. It was as if she had radar for alcohol. Finally, they settled into a kind of tacit agreement, a truce. She stopped admonishing him, and he made an effort to appear normal. There was tension in the house and Ryan spent as much time away from home as possible. When they were together, they tried to be civil with one another, but every now and then an argument would erupt. It was like a brush fire. It would flair up suddenly and needed to be put down as soon as possible.

Preparations began for the Christmas season. The artificial tree, which had been stored in the attic, was taken out of the box and Emma assembled it in the living room— just as she did last year and the year before that, and all the years since their children were born. Before the birth of Jaime, Emma and Ryan used a real Christmas tree; one they cut themselves from their eighty-acre parcel. But after Jaime arrived and was diagnosed with allergies and asthma, the real Christmas tree had to go. A new, artificial one was purchased. Once erected, it was still a beautiful tree. It just took a little more imagination. There were ornaments which had pictures of the girls when they were babies. Other ornaments had pictures when the children were older. The newest had pictures of grandchildren. There were special dated commemorative ornaments purchased throughout the years.

All in all, there were lots of decorations. Every year, Emma added a few more to the assortment. Both she and Ryan looked forward to the annual event of decorating the tree. When the work was finished and the tree was resplendent with all the decorations, it added a sense of warmth and well-being to the room. It was almost a cheerful atmosphere, and it would be again when the children came.

They arrived three days before Christmas Eve. For Jamie, it was an easy trip to make. She lived only twelve miles away in her apartment in New Jericho. Ruthie and her family drove all the way from Texas. It took them three days. She and her husband, Michael, had two boys, ages 7 and 5, and a four-month-old baby girl. For Ryan and Emma it was the first time to meet Allison, the new baby. Emma and Ryan were so excited to have everyone together again in the house, they forgot anything was wrong between them.

All Christmases are special, but this one was extra special, with the family all together again. An obligatory trip was made to Frankenmuth so everyone could visit Bronner's, the world's largest Christmas store, and get their commemorative Christmas ornament. It needed to be marked with this year's date to make it special. That way they would each have one to remind them of this particular Christmas. It would be Allison's first ornament.

There were so many things to do, and so little time. After the shopping at Bronner's, Ryan took the grandchildren to the water park in Frankenmuth. The following day, Ryan took them to the pond so they could go ice fishing. He had built a small makeshift shanty so the boys could stay warm. The two little boys had a terrific time, as most of the activities were centered around them. One night, the family climbed into the van and Emma drove them into New Jericho to look at the Christmas lights. She wouldn't permit Ryan to drive.

"We have precious cargo—our children and grandchildren. I will drive."

Ryan didn't object. He quietly slipped into a seat in the back of the van.

One house had an elaborate display with a life-sized, plastic horse pulling a sled containing a Santa Claus figure and a huge pile of presents. The house was completely covered in strands of Christmas lights; there must have been thousands of light bulbs.

On Christmas morning, bright and early, everyone awoke to exchange gifts. Presents were given and everybody was joyful. The Christmas spirit was in the air and neither Jamie nor Ruth had any idea of tension between their parents. The animosity between Ryan and Emma was well hidden. Erik and Josh, Ruthie's two little boys, received an obscene amount of presents.

Later Emma, with the help of her two daughters, prepared the family feast. They cooked turkey with stuffing, ham, sweet potatoes, mashed potatoes, green vegetables, corn, and for dessert, a choice of cheesecake or strawberry shortcake. Ryan and Michael had a helping of each. Everyone went away from the table stuffed and feeling lethargic. After a suitable rest period, as one of the children put it "to revolve," the family members played board games, including Candy Land and Monopoly.

"You really shouldn't have given them so much," Ruthie said. "You are spoiling them rotten."

"But we want to," Emma replied. "That's what grandparents are for."

"Well, you'd better enjoy them," Ruthie said. "You're going to be around them for two more weeks. You will find that they are consistently on the move. They never get tired. They just keep running around, going from one thing to the other, and demanding to be entertained constantly."

"Oh... I hadn't noticed."

"Eventually they drop from exhaustion at bedtime. But their demands can be beyond your capacity to endure. They can make life difficult."

"That's okay," Emma said. "We've been

looking forward to your visit for months. We can rest after you leave."

"I bet you won't feel that way after another week."

"Maybe, but I believe we will."

13

Three days after Christmas, Ryan slipped away from home. Everyone was busy with their own activities and no one noticed when he left. He went straight to Lilly's cottage.

"Merry Christmas," he said when he saw her. He handed her a box of Russell Stover chocolates.

"Oh, that's very sweet of you," she said, accepting his gift. "It's been a while. I didn't know whether or not I'd ever see you again."

"I still need a birthday present for Emma. Remember, I talked about buying one of your paintings." Ryan grinned, looking sheepish, pretending the whole painting thing wasn't a ruse—just an excuse so he could see her again. If Lilly was aware of that, she didn't show it. She was either too polite or she didn't care.

"The last time you were here you fell asleep and when you awoke you were in a hurry to leave. Remember?"

"Yes, I do. What was in that tea of yours?"

"Oh, I don't know. A little bit of this, and

a little bit of that."

"Seriously, what is in your... how did you call it, your anti-melancholy/have-a-nice-day brew?"

"Well, if you must know, I start with tea, plain, ordinary pekoe tea. Then I add some herbs, in correct proportions. Proportions are everything. Let's see. I use dandelion root, which is good to stimulate the liver as well as the gall bladder, chicory to smooth it out, a bit of thorn apple, a pinch of mandragora, and just a smidgen of henbane."

"And you get all that from the super market?"

"No, silly, it comes from my garden. I grow everything organically. I don't use pesticides. So if that is what concerns you, you don't need to worry."

"I'm not worried. I know about dandelions because I have them all over my front yard in June. I can't get rid of them. The other stuff I'm not familiar with, but I guess it works. I sure didn't feel melancholy."

"The tea is supposed to relax you. I hope you had a nice day."

"I did, very nice. I remember that I have never been quite that relaxed before. But I don't recall if you said I could buy a painting or not. Would you sell me one?"

"No, silly, I won't sell you a painting. I will give you one. That's why I placed the pile of pictures in front of you. The ones you used for a pillow. The idea was to pick out a painting you wanted to keep."

"That's sweet of you, but I really couldn't accept one without paying."

"Oh, you'll pay." She smiled a devious smile. "But the problem is I don't accept cash. It's a house rule, so this one's a gift. I will be hurt if you reject my offer."

"Well, in that case.... Can I ask you a question?"

"Of course. Would you like some tea?"

"No, thank you. Not today. I want to stay awake. I need to be at the university later and I want to be clear-headed."

"Isn't the university closed for Christmas break?"

"Well, yes. It is closed, but I am behind in my work and I need to catch up."

"I see," Lilly said smiling. She tossed her head, shaking her hair.

God, Ryan thought, *she's so beautiful. Breathtaking.*

She walked up to Ryan, getting especially close, and put her head close to his. "Something is different. I smell... innocence... new life...an absence of sin. There must a baby at your house?"

"Yes, how did you know? Ruthie brought her baby. She's my daughter from Texas. It's her third child and the whole family is visiting with Emma and me for a couple of weeks."

"How lovely." She was still standing so close to Ryan that he could smell her perfume. It was a pleasant sensation; the aroma was of flowers. Ryan found it intoxicating. He could feel his heart flutter, and felt weak in the knees.

"So you are a grandpa?"

"I already was a grandpa," Ryan was barely able to respond. The effort was difficult.

"Would you like to pick out a painting now, or do you want to wait until later?" She put her face right up to his.

"We can wait," Ryan stammered.

"Maybe you could give me partial payment now."

"What do you mean? I thought it was a

gift?"

She kissed him and Ryan responded. "That's the payment I was looking for," she said playfully. Lilly pulled off her t-shirt, revealing her full breasts, her nipples erect. Ryan stared at her for a moment, and then removed his shirt. She took his hand and led him to the bedroom. There was a queen-sized bed. The shades on the windows were pulled almost completely down letting in only a tiny amount of light.

They removed the rest of their clothing and fell together onto the bed. For the next few minutes they made intense, passionate love. She drew him into her, and he had the sensation that he was falling, being sucked into a whirling tornado. He and Lilly were snakes. Serpents entwined and twisting together in a breeding-ball, a wild frenzy of delight.

Ryan had never experienced anything like it. It wasn't like making love to Emma, or anyone else, including Heather. It was better. It was like all the women he had ever known, added together and then multiplied to the tenth power. He didn't think it was possible to experience such bliss. It was a feeling of total surrender, complete abandonment and ecstasy. He thought it was almost a supernatural experience.

When they finished, they lay together without speaking. Both were covered in perspiration. After a few minutes, Lilly turned to him and said in a voice that was a perfect imitation of the old actress, Marlene Dietrich, "This might be a good time for a smoke, darling. You wouldn't happen to have a cigarette on you, would you, darling?"

"I'm sorry," Ryan said. "I don't smoke."

"Pity. Tobacco is such a deliciously wicked vice."

They remained silent for a few more moments and then Ryan said, "Lilly, I am curious. It's about the old woman, the one you referred to as Granny Blue. Mr. Metcalf thinks those paintings of yours were painted by the old woman."

"I know he does."

"How does that come to happen? I mean, why doesn't he know the truth?"

"What is the truth? It's a game, darling." She was continuing to use her Marlene Dietrich voice. "It's fun. Granny Blue and I play this game sometime. She's a witch, you know. It gives her pleasure to deceive people. It, how do you say, gets her off. That's what witches do. Besides, we don't see any harm in the game. I encourage her. It helps to keep people away."

"Don't you want people to appreciate your art?"

"Some people, yes. People like you, but not everyone. People can be tedious."

"Lilly, I'm not an art critic. In fact, I don't know much about art. But it seems to me that you are extraordinarily accomplished for someone so young. Your work looks like it was done by a master like Rembrandt, or Michelangelo or someone of that caliber."

"He was my teacher."

"Who?"

"Michelangelo. You see, like him, I was born with a gift." Her voice returned to normal, and she lost the Bavarian accent.

"That's an understatement."

"Ryan, darling, what was the question you wanted to ask me?"

"It was about the old lady."

"The witch?"

"Yes, if that's what you want to call her. But to be honest, it doesn't seem nice to insult her by name-calling. I mean, she's old and that word seems… disrespectful. The elderly should be treated with respect. That's one of my core principles."

"Yes, Ryan, of course you're right. I shouldn't be disrespectful. It's my sense of humor. I like to poke fun at her because she's so doting and confused. I find the old hag amusing."

"Whose idea was it to play your game of deception? Was it your idea or the old lady's?"

"It was her idea, Ryan. That's the kind of thing she loves to do. She always says, 'Keep them guessing.' These games keep her alive and vigorous. Otherwise her life would be too boring."

Ryan remembered the word *boring* from his last visit. He hoped it wouldn't set off a repetition of that scene. "You wouldn't think at her advanced age she would need to play games. She looks about two steps from needing assisted living."

"Don't worry about her. Looks can be deceiving. Granny Blue is a feisty old bird who can take care of herself. Believe me, I know."

Lilly peeled the covers back and stepped out of bed, revealing her naked body. She stood there in front of Ryan like a model, allowing him to gaze at her. Her body was perfect in every way—without flaw or blemish. She had no cellulite or sagging, only hard, firm flesh. She knew it and stood without shame in her nakedness, smiling down at Ryan, allowing him to admire her. Finally, after what seemed to Ryan to be an unusually long time, she stepped into her underpants and slipped on her tee shirt.

Ryan was enthralled. He had never in his life beheld anything so beautiful and at the same time so exciting. She could have been a Greek statue, except she wasn't made of marble. She was real, and alive. Ryan couldn't believe his good fortune. *This is what I needed for Christmas. This was her present to me. Now I know what it's like to live.*

Lilly walked from the room and returned holding a painting. It was a picture of a deer standing in the forest and looking directly at the viewer. "Perhaps this one," Lilly said. "I believe your wife likes nature scenes?"

"Yes, I believe so. To be honest, I don't

really know."

"Well, I like it. I think she will like it. Why don't you take it to her and we'll see."

"Okay," Ryan said, still a little stupefied from the best sex of his entire life. "Whatever you think."

"I think it will grab her. Ryan, there's a shower in the bathroom. You might want to take one, professor, if you are going back to school."

"Thank you, Lilly. I will."

14

It was early morning in the Dennison home. Emma and Ryan were sleeping, but suddenly awoke to the shrill call of their daughter, Ruthie.

"Mom… Dad… come quick!" There was the sound of desperation in Ruthie's voice.

"Ruthie," Emma yelled, jumping from the bed. "What is it, honey? What's wrong?"

"The baby. She won't wake up. Oh my God, Michael, do something."

Ryan and Emma threw on their robes and raced to the guest room that Ruthie, Michael, and the baby occupied. Ruthie and Michael were standing by the crib. Emma and Ryan saw Ruthie was holding baby Allison, and gently shaking her. The baby's head wobbled and her little arms and legs dangled at her side.

"Oh my God," Emma said, "Is she all right? Is she breathing? Hold her head up Ruthie. Don't let it dangle like that. Check her breathing."

"Mom, Dad," Ruthie cried, "I can't feel

anything." Ruthie's husband, Michael, took the baby and examined her, but the infant didn't move. There was no response.

"Michael," Ryan demanded, "Give her CPR. Emma, call 911."

Emma went to make the call, just as the two little boys entered the room.

"Not now!" Ruthie screamed. "Go back to bed." The boys turned and scrambled back to their bedroom.

The ambulance arrived fifteen minutes later. Nothing had changed with respect to the baby's condition. Michael kept trying to give CPR and when he tired, Ryan took over. The women cried. Michael cried. The only one able to keep their composure and remain level-headed throughout the ordeal was Ryan.

The baby was examined by the emergency medical team and efforts were made to revive the infant. At 6:25 a.m., Allison was pronounced dead. One of the EMTs explained that the police would be called and would arrive shortly to take everyone's statement. "An autopsy will have to be performed. When a death is unexplained, like what happened to your baby, the law requires that an autopsy be done to determine the cause of death."

"I got up to give Allison her early morning feeding," Ruthie whimpered. "I thought she was sleeping. I didn't know anything was wrong until I lifted her."

"I understand," the EMT said. "There are certain procedures in a situation like this that we must follow. We will take the baby back with us to the hospital. Try and get yourselves composed as much as possible. It's a terrible tragedy and you have our condolences. The police will be here shortly."

Ruthie was so wracked with grief, she could barely stand by herself. Emma held her up to keep her from collapsing. While she was comforting Ruthie, Emma noticed a man sitting in the cab of the ambulance. Apparently he was the driver, because he didn't come out of the vehicle like the other people did. There was something familiar about him, but Emma couldn't figure what it was. Everything was happening so quickly.

A few minutes later, the police arrived and the family had to relive the tragedy and answer a lot of questions.

***

Three days later, the Dennisons and a few family friends attended the funeral for baby Allison.

It was a crisp winter day and snow was falling softly. The minister was a local man named Robert Bunting. He was pastor of the New Jericho Community Church. Pastor Bunting was a young man who looked to be fresh out of seminary. He addressed the mourners: "In the *First Book of Thessalonians*, Chapter 4, God tells us that if we believe that Jesus died and rose again, then those who sleep in Jesus, God will bring with Him into heaven."

He paused so the mourners could reflect on his words. "The Apostle Paul, a man who was well acquainted with suffering, tells us in the *Book of Philippians*, that to die in Christ is gain. What does it mean? It means that your beloved little one, Allison, is not lost to you forever. She is absent from the body, but present with the Lord. You are parted only temporarily, for a brief while. You have the hope—no, not the hope—you have the certainty, that you will hold your precious dear one again in your arms when you meet in heaven.

"Although we grieve for baby Allison, we should not let our grief overwhelm us. We should not let it weigh us down and prevent us from living. Rather, let us celebrate Allison's short, sweet life, knowing that we will see her again in heaven. She is with her Maker, she is in a safe place. She is with God.

"It is we who must continue. We who will have to endure such things as failure, disappointment, pain, and heartbreak. Why? Because these things are the prices we pay for the privilege of being alive. So my friends, when you leave here today, I beseech you— don't go under a cloud of despair. No matter how much grief you feel today, leave your anguish at the cemetery gates. Remember Allison. Cherish her memory, and take comfort in the knowledge she resides with the Lord.

"As we are often reminded, dust we are, and to dust we shall return. Let me end with the Good News, as I read the fourth chapter of *First Thessalonians*, versus 16 and 17." Pastor Bunting raised his Bible and began to read: "For the Lord Himself shall descend from heaven with a shout, with the voice of the archangel, and with the trump of God: and the dead in Christ shall rise first. Then we which are alive and remain shall be caught up together with them in the cloud, to meet the Lord in the air: and so shall we ever be with the Lord. Wherefore comfort one another with these words. Amen."

15

Two months after Allison's funeral and the atmosphere in the house remained gloomy. The official cause of death was listed as SIDS (Sudden Infant Death Syndrome). Ruthie and Michael and the two boys were back home in Texas. Emma was devastated by the tragedy. Ryan was heartsick too, but he didn't shut down like Emma. He seemed preoccupied. One day he went on a 3-day bender. Jaime found him in town and brought him home. After that episode, Ryan would sometimes disappear and stay away for a day or two. Sometimes he would return to the house drunk, and then he would cry.

Emma had looked forward to the visit with her children for so long. It had been a glorious Christmas, but the visit ended so tragically. Depressed, she moped around the house, beyond acting as if everything was normal. It wasn't. It never would be. Emma was miserable; a shadow of her former self. She stopped eating and her weight dropped by ten pounds. Emma's misery was apparent to everyone who saw her.

It was March 2nd, Emma's birthday. Ryan thought maybe the two of them could reconnect emotionally and celebrate. It might cheer her up a little. It was certainly worth a try.

"I have a surprise for you," Ryan said. He left the room and returned holding a large bag which contained the painting wrapped in paper. Emma tore off the paper and gazed at the painting.

"Thank you," she muttered. "It's thoughtful of you." She did not change the expression on her face.

"You're welcome. Happy birthday, sweetheart. Is there something special you would like to do today?" Ryan waited for a reply. Nothing. No response from Emma whatsoever. He expected something. He wanted a little enthusiasm or gratitude, some expression of emotion. "What's wrong, Emma? Don't you like my gift?"

Emma didn't answer. She just sat staring at the painting. Tears began to flow from her eyes. She didn't speak.

"I don't understand. You told me what a great painter she was. I thought you'd like it.

It's a nature scene."

"I know it's a nature scene," Emma said softly. "I can see that, and I recognize the animal."

"What? What are you talking about? It's just a painting, Emma, nothing more. It's a picture of a deer."

Emma wiped her face with a napkin. "Yes, Ryan, I know. But it's that deer."

"What?"

"It's the deer that was in our garden. The one the hunter was chasing that day last winter. Remember, the man who saw the girl in the forest? He didn't think she was wearing a coat, and he shot our fence. Remember the visit by the DNR ranger? Well, the deer in the picture is the same deer. The nine-point antlers give it away. That, and the look in its eye. Once you've seen that look, you don't forget it. I tell you, Ryan, it's that same goddamn deer."

"Emma, that's not true. Your imagination is running away with you. I've noticed these days it tends to do that. It's just a picture of a deer. Do you know how many deer there are in Michigan? There must be millions."

"I don't care. The number of deer in

Michigan is irrelevant. I only know there is one particular deer. He and I have an understanding."

"Emma, I don't know what you are talking about. Do you like the picture or not?"

"Ryan, let me be honest with you." Emma wiped her eyes. "I am heartbroken. I am a woman who is suffering. I lost my grandchild. My daughter, our daughter, is grief-stricken. I don't know if she will ever recover. I don't feel like celebrating, especially not on my birthday. I feel like crying. And you give me a picture of a deer—that deer. There's something wrong with that picture. I'm surprised you can't see it. I feel like the deer is mocking us. I don't know why. All I know is I don't want to look at it, and I don't want it hanging on our wall looking at me."

"Lilly thought you'd like it."

"Lilly! Who cares what Lilly thought? Who is she anyway? What do we know about her? She's a young, silly woman who can draw well and speaks in riddles. She lives alone in the middle of the woods. Or she lives with some old woman who is impolite and unfriendly. Is Lilly employed? Does she earn her subsistence from her artwork? Does she take care of the old lady, or does the old lady take care of her?

"Who knows? Who cares? Not me, I don't care. I have more important things on my mind these days than that foolish girl. But thank you, Ryan. It was a nice try and I know you meant well, but I am still grieving and I don't know how long it's going to take me to recover. I guess I wasn't able to leave my grief at the cemetery gate. And then there's you, and your problem. I am referring to your inability to stop drinking. You're not much of a support system, Ryan, especially when I am grieving. So you see, I might never stop crying."

Emma stood and picked up the picture. She walked to the bedroom. "I'm going to take a nap," she said. She closed the bedroom door behind her. Inside the bedroom, by herself, she covered the painting with a towel and placed it against the wall in the closet.

***

A month and a half later, spring finally arrived and everything turned green. Emma was beginning to feel better. She started to jog again. She purchased a sling-shot from the sports supply store and a bag of white marbles. She tied them from her belt along with a can of pepper spray. There had been no sightings of wolves in their woods—not any. Emma didn't want to take chances. If that wolf, or dog, or whatever it was came near her, she would be prepared. Ryan had previously gone out on several occasions carrying a shotgun looking for the wolf, but he never encountered it. He even put out a large Have-a-Heart trap, hoping the animal might be hungry enough to get caught. To date, the trap netted two raccoons, a possum, and one skunk—no wolves. Emma came to believe that maybe the animal she saw in the forest was just a dog after all; some pet from somewhere beyond their property that ran away from home and headed into the forest—a random event.

And yet, there was that old woman. Emma thought about her a lot while she jogged through the woods. *Did she really say the things to me I thought she said? Could I have imagined it? Why would that old woman pretend that she was the painter when she wasn't? What kind of a twisted, perverted mind does the old lady have?*

And then, one afternoon, while Emma was jogging through the woods, she thought about her birthday present from Ryan. *I hate that painting*, she thought. *I don't want it in my closet. I don't want it anywhere. I'm taking it back to the gallery.* She turned around and ran back to the house. "Ryan," she called out. "Ryan, are you here? Where are you?" He wasn't there. Less than an hour ago he had been sitting in the kitchen reading the newspaper. Now he was gone, again, and he didn't even have the courtesy to leave a note.

Lately, Emma thought, *he has been missing a lot. Where does he go? He can't be at the university all the time.* Emma wondered. *What is he doing? He's probably at some bar. Oh well,* she thought, *I don't need him. Let him drink.* She changed her clothes, grabbed the painting, jumped into her car, and headed to town.

***

Emma arrived at the Amanita Gallery and noticed the wooden sign hanging over the door. The sign was painted on a weathered piece of planking. The wood had turned grey and on either side of the words indicating the gallery's name were pictures of mushrooms—white ones, with polka dots on red caps.

When she entered the gallery, it appeared deserted. There were no customers present and it was quiet except for some very soft elevator-type music playing in the background. The first thing that grabbed her attention was the large, orange picture *The Tree of Hope*. She looked to see if the poison ivy vines were still in the picture. Yep, still there. She wondered if the vines had always been in the picture. Was this just another example of her mind playing tricks on her? Maybe she had just imagined when she saw the painting for the first time that no vines were in the picture.

She turned away from the painting and yelled, "Hello... is someone here?" She heard a sound from a back room and then the gentleman appeared. He was the same man she had spoken with before who had introduced himself as Mr. Metcalf. He was dressed as he was the other times she had seen him—a suit that didn't fit properly, a white shirt and bow tie.

"Can I help you?" Mr. Metcalf asked.

"Yes. I've brought one of your paintings back. I wish to return it, and I was wondering if I would be entitled to a refund, or at least a partial refund."

"May I see the painting?"

"It's a picture of a deer. It was painted by Lilith." She walked over to the counter and placed the painting on it.

Mr. Metcalf looked at the picture. "I'm sorry," he said. "I don't believe this painting came from our gallery."

"What do you mean?" Emma asked.

"I mean it was probably purchased from somewhere else, maybe in town from another gallery. I know the artist, of course, but not this particular work. It has never been in our inventory or displayed here. In fact, this is the first time I have ever seen this work. It's quite good, but all of her work is good."

"Really? You've never seen it before?"

"No, I promise you, I have never seen it. Are you certain you bought it here?"

"Actually, I didn't buy it. It was a gift. I just assumed it came from here."

"I'm sorry, it didn't."

Emma hesitated. She thought about what to do with the picture. Then she said, "Mr. Metcalf, do you think the painting is worth anything?"

"Of course."

"Would you like to buy it from me?"

"You don't want to keep it?"

"No, Mr. Metcalf, I don't. I'll tell you what. I'll sell it to you for ten dollars. Maybe you can sell it to someone else for more money. I don't know what these things bring and I really don't care. As far as I'm concerned, I'll be happy with ten bucks. It will pay for my gas. What do you say?"

"That would be stealing the painting from you and I am not comfortable doing that. It wouldn't be right. But if you don't want it, I will give you $200 for the painting."

"You do know who painted this picture?"

"Yes, I already told you that."

"You think it was that feeble old lady, the one with the walker, and the oxygen tank, don't you?"

"Yes, I do—Lilith."

"What would you say if I told you that old lady didn't really paint it? The real artist is about twenty years old. She's the one who lives out there by herself in the woods. She doesn't walk with a walker and she's not on oxygen. She's a very healthy young girl and she's got some kind of weird game going with the old lady. They're in cahoots together. She paints the pictures and the old lady pretends to be the artist and claims the credit."

"Why would she do that?"

"I haven't a clue. Maybe because the old woman is practically blind. I don't know. Why does anyone do what they do?"

"It just seems a little strange. I'm sorry, lady... I can't recall your name. But I find that a hard story to believe."

"That's understandable. Nevertheless, it's true."

"Whatever you say, madam." He began to rub the back of his ear. He seemed unaware of the gesture. "Do you wish to sell your painting?"

"Yeah, I do."

"I will go to the other room and fetch my checkbook."

After Emma received her payment and was about to leave the gallery, she stopped again in front of *The Tree of Hope*. It really was an incredible painting. She had to admire the artist, whoever it was. She looked at the babies budding out of the tree. They reminded her of the Christmas ornaments she had on her Christmas tree. Babies all look alike, she thought. These babies all looked similar except for subtle, tiny differences making each face unique. Then Emma noticed one face that looked familiar. She stared at the picture as the room began to spin around her. She could feel her legs give out beneath her as she crumpled to the floor. The last word she uttered was "Allison."

16

Emma wasn't unconscious for long. Mr. Metcalf had smelling salts and she was revived quickly. She apologized for fainting and didn't tell the truth as to why she had collapsed. She pooh-poohed the entire episode and told Mr. Metcalf she hadn't eaten all day and something about her blood sugar. He wanted to call 911, but she insisted it wasn't necessary. Driving home, her mind raced in all directions. *I must make a plan,* she thought, *I need to remain calm and figure out what is happening to me. What is going on? Do I need a psychiatrist?*

She planned to tell Ryan over dinner. But as usual, he wasn't home when he was supposed to be. She sat on the couch, waiting for her husband, and getting more and more annoyed. She knew he wasn't teaching an evening class this night, so where could he be?

Then she remembered Heather. It had been ten years. Heather was a young girl, a student of his, who had become infatuated with him. She followed him around like a puppy. It started innocently enough. She would come to his office for advising and to make plans for her academic career. Later, the relationship changed, and she and Ryan became friends. She would come to his office just to chat. Then they started having lunches together. And then.... It took Emma a long time to figure out what was going on between her husband and his student, Heather. It was Jamie, who first alerted Emma to Ryan's shenanigans. Jamie had seen Ryan and Heather together at the Wagon Wheel Tavern, drinking and behaving foolishly.

"Honestly, Mother. You should have seen them. It was embarrassing. They were all lovey-dovey like a couple of dewy-eyed teenagers. It made me want to throw up. I considered confronting him directly, but I didn't. I just slipped out of the tavern and came home. I thought about it. He is my father and has two daughters. How can he do this to me and Ruthie and to you? After thinking about it for a while, I decided I should tell you. I thought you needed to know."

"Thank you, Jamie, I'll deal with it. I'm not sure how, but I'll think of something."

As it happened, Emma didn't have to deal with it because the following day Dr. Dennison was reprimanded by his department chairman and told his behavior with Heather had been reported. If he wanted to keep his job, he had better terminate his relationship with the student immediately. Ryan denied everything, of course, saying it was all innocent and misinterpreted. Despite his protestations, his application for promotion was denied.

Apparently, Ryan felt he was in love and the world wasn't treating him fairly. He found relief through alcohol. Heather didn't want to quit the relationship so the two of them rented an apartment together. Actually, Ryan rented the apartment; Heather just moved in. It was their secret love-nest, where Heather lived and Ryan found a little afternoon delight. But they couldn't keep their secret for long. They were outed by another student who inadvertently informed on them one day when chatting with the department secretary.

But all that was in the past. Ryan had almost lost his job over the incident. That was when he started going to meetings of

Alcoholics Anonymous. After a few years, things returned somewhat to normal.

Now, it appeared to Emma, the black days, as she referred to them, were back. Although this time, it is not Heather. Who could it be? It must be that girl—Lilly.

Emma thought she knew what needed to be done. She would start with her digital camera. She would go to the gallery and take a photograph of *The Tree of Hope*. She knew the sign on the wall said no photographs, but she didn't care. She would document the painting, to show how sweet little Allison, her deceased granddaughter, was budding from the tree. Lilith had no right to use Allison's image. It was beyond disrespectful. It was macabre.

Emma could show the picture to her soon-to-be psychiatrist so he could confirm whether or not she was crazy. She didn't believe she was. Also, she might be able to demonstrate how the picture changed over time. Maybe it was still changing. If so, she would have proof. She could take pictures over intervals of time and provide evidence she wasn't imagining things.

When Ryan finally returned home, he was

somewhat intoxicated, but not drunk. Emma was disgusted.

"I need to talk to you, preferably when you are sober, but if that's not possible then now will have to do."

"I only had a few drinks."

"Whatever. I need to tell you something about that painting."

"Your birthday present?"

"No, Ryan, not that painting. The other one. *The Tree of Hope.*"

"All right, what about it?"

"It has Allison's face on it."

"What?"

"Allison, our granddaughter. She is budding out of that tree."

"You sound like a lunatic, Emma. Have you lost your marbles?"

"Okay, don't believe me. So come to town with me and I will show you."

"We can't go to town, it's too late. The gallery is closed."

"Okay, then go with me in the morning."

"Fine, Emma, we'll go tomorrow. But to be honest I'm getting sick of all this hocus-pocus, mumbo jumbo stuff about paintings. First it was a painting of a wolf that was sold to a Wolf. Imagine the probability. Then, there was the deer picture, which by the way wasn't so easy for me to obtain, and which you summarily rejected and stuck in the closet. You know, that hurt my feelings. And now this one, which I might point out to you, had to have been painted before Allison was even born. How do you explain that?"

"I can't. But if you didn't buy the picture from the Amanita Gallery, then how did you come by it?"

"I went to Lilly's house. Are you satisfied? I went there by myself and told her your birthday was approaching, and she gave it to me to give to you for a present."

"She gave it to you—for free?"

"Yes, Emma, for free. Gratis. Without cost. That's what friends do."

"So now she's your friend? How long have you been visiting her?"

"A while, Emma, it's been a few times. She's a remarkable young woman and I find her to be pleasant company."

"I bet you do. Is she a friend like Heather was a friend?"

"She's not a student. Stop interrogating me. I'm a grown man."

"I guess you're not going to your meetings?"

"Temporarily. I've been busy lately. But believe me, I'm under control. I can manage things myself."

"I see that," Emma said. She stomped out of the room.

***

The following morning Ryan and Emma were still testy with one another and barely on speaking terms. Nevertheless, they got into the car and drove to New Jericho. Mr. Metcalf was just opening the gallery when they arrived. As soon as Mr. Metcalf left the room Emma reached into her pocketbook and took out her camera. She snapped a picture of *The Tree of Hope*. Then she put the camera back into her pocketbook and said to Ryan, "See? Can you see, right over here?" She pointed to the image of one of the babies. It's Allison. Can't you see the resemblance?"

"It's a baby," Ryan answered. "A generic baby. It looks like all the other babies."

"No, this one is different. It is Allison."

Ryan stared at the painting. He studied it carefully. After a few moments, he said, "Emma, maybe there is a slight resemblance; perhaps, I don't know. It could simply be coincidence. It could be the lighting. It's just an image like the others and, as we both know, all babies look alike. Have you ever thought there's the possibility that you are suggestible? You are easily influenced, like the placebo effect. Maybe you see Allison's image because you want to see her."

"You can't see it? You can't see the resemblance?"

"No, Emma, I can't. I'm sorry."

Just then, Mr. Metcalf came back into the room. "Can I be of help?"

"No, thank you," Ryan said. "We were just admiring the painting."

"Yes, it's quite a work of art. Many people come just to admire it. Repeat customers. It's very popular."

"Understandably," Ryan said.

Mr. Metcalf turned and walked away. "If you need anything, just call."

"I'm going to look at the other pictures," Ryan said, as he turned and walked away from Emma. She remained where she stood, transfixed, staring at *The Tree of Hope*. In a few moments Ryan returned. "Emma, come here; I want to show you something." She followed him into the adjacent room. Hanging on one of the walls was the picture of the deer—her birthday present. "Can you explain this?" Ryan asked Emma.

"I sold it."

"You sold your birthday present?"

"Yes, Ryan. I sold it. I didn't tell you because I didn't want to hurt your feelings. Besides, I didn't see the point in telling you. I took the money and bought clothes. I needed them. I thought you would want me to have something I liked for my present, so I sold it to Mr. Metcalf. I took the money and bought something I wanted."

Ryan stared at her intently. His mouth was puckered and Emma thought he might be grinding his teeth. He sometimes did that when he was really angry. Finally Ryan said, "I feel badly for what you did to Lilly. She was only being nice."

"What I did to Lilly? You're kidding. I didn't do anything to Lilly. I don't know her. She's not my friend—she's yours."

"You don't deserve that picture. What

will I tell Lilly? She's a sensitive girl."

Emma smiled and then chuckled. "I'll bet she is," she said sarcastically. "What does she have, about a hundred-thousand paintings? She's going to miss this one picture—the one she gave to you for free. I'm sure she'll be devastated, just heartbroken. Tell her anything you want, just give me a fucking break!"

Ryan failed to understand Emma's contempt or appreciate her sarcasm. He was so angry his fists were clenched. First his present was rejected, and now she was mocking him.

"Come," he said. "Let's go home."

17

Yes, the black days were certainly back. Once again, Ryan was missing and Emma was left at home alone imagining where he had gone. She went about her routine, as if nothing was out of the ordinary. She fed her birds, did her housework, jogged a little, and watched some television. She suspected her husband was with Lilly at her cottage in the woods. She also realized they were probably having an affair. Strangely, she didn't care. *Lilly can have him. Let her try and keep him sober.* Yet, the more she thought about her errant husband, the more curious she got. *Why was Lilly interested in him?* There had to be a thirty-year age difference between Ryan and Lilly.

And then there was the matter of that serpent-tongued old woman. What role did she have to play in this drama? The more Emma thought about her, the more she realized that no matter what Lilly had previously told her, the old lady must be the real artist. She had to be. Lilly was simply too young. Yes, she had drawing ability, that couldn't be denied, but it was a long way from sketching with charcoal to painting pictures like those hanging in the gallery. It would take a lifetime to acquire the kind of skills needed to paint like that—a lifetime much longer than the one lived by that little girl in the woods. Of course, Emma realized, it was remotely possible that Lilly was a prodigy; someone like Mozart—self-trained, and born with the innate ability to compose music. That was unlikely. Whatever it was, Emma was angry and she was determined to get to the bottom of the mystery.

She needed to get out of the house. It was associated with too many bad memories— the death of the baby and her husband's behavior. She wanted to be somewhere she was comfortable; a place where she could think. She wanted somewhere quiet so she could sort out her feelings. In the past, whenever she felt this way she would instinctively head to the library. The library was associated with pleasant memories. It had been so since her college days when she majored in Library Science at the University of Tennessee. Back then, she planned to become a librarian. That never happened because she met Ryan, married, and started a family. But the library still held a special appeal to her. It was a refuge. She grabbed her coat and headed to the public library.

***

The library had a large selection of coffee-table books. Emma grabbed a few and sat at a table. She was trying to get her mind temporarily off her problems. She would deal with those later. The atmosphere of the library was comforting and just what Emma needed.

She started browsing through the first book. She didn't read the text, but merely looked at the pictures. The book was entitled *Nomads of Niger* and it was about a nomadic people called the *Wodaabe* who live in sub-Saharan Africa. The photographs were spectacular and documented the life and festivals of an extraordinary people.

The second book she opened was entitled *Dreams of India*. It was written by a photo-journalist named Raghu Rai. The book was filled with photographs taken over a twenty-year period of time which captured the unique images of this exotic and beautiful land. *How I would like to see these places,* Emma thought. *If only I could go there. Wouldn't that be the experience of a lifetime?*

The third book was an enormous volume entitled, *Great Works of Art.* The book was compiled by James Kenneth Goldfeder and contained pictures of great art treasures from around the world. Emma browsed about a third of the way through the book when an illustration caught her eye. It was entitled *The Tree of Hope* and the artist's name was Lilith. Emma read the caption beneath the illustration. The work was done in 1733. It went missing in 1942, presumably plundered by the Nazis. After the war, the painting was recovered and currently hangs in the Kunsthistorisches Museum (The Kunst) in Vienna, Austria. *Will you look at that!*

Emma couldn't believe her discovery. She made a photocopy of the page and left the library, heading straight to the Amanita Gallery. There were a few patrons in the gallery, but as soon as the last one left the building, Emma called out to the manager.

"Mr. Metcalf, I want to show you

something."

The man recognized her. "Do you have another painting you want to sell?"

"No, sir, but I would like to get your thoughts on something." She handed him the photocopy.

Mr. Metcalf looked at the picture, but showed no emotion. "Interesting," was all he said.

"Well, what do you think it means?"

"I think it means there is more than one version of the painting. Maybe Lilith copied it. I wouldn't be alarmed."

"She copied the artist's name, also?"

"Perhaps. I don't know. Maybe they have the same name. It could be a coincidence. The painting is not exactly the same picture. There are no vines hanging from the tree in the older version."

"Really? I hadn't noticed." Emma took the paper back from Mr. Metcalf and compared it to the one on the wall. He was right. They weren't exactly the same; similar, but a tiny bit different.

"And," Mr. Metcalf continued, "there are fewer babies in the original picture than there are in ours."

Sure enough, Mr. Metcalf was correct again. Emma tried to see if she could make out Allison's face, but even though the picture in the photocopy was tiny, Emma could tell Allison's image wasn't there. *It's like a Rorschach Inkblot Test,* she thought, *you see what you want to see. Ryan might have been right.* "Isn't it unethical to copy another person's picture and call it your own?"

"It happens. Besides, we're not sure that is what occurred. Lilith may have an explanation. She's the one you should talk with, not me."

"By Lilith, you mean the old lady?"

"That's correct."

"I still want to meet her. Do you think it could be arranged?"

"I can try. She is due to come here Wednesday. If you like, I will try and set up an appointment for you. If you leave your telephone number, I will call you."

"Thank you, Mr. Metcalf, I would like that very much." She took a pen and paper from her pocketbook and wrote down her information.

Lilith

***

It's hard to determine the exact moment a marriage is finished. For Emma, it was shortly after she returned home from visiting the library and gallery. Despite the bad feelings she had toward her husband, she was looking forward to showing him the picture she found at the library. She was sure Ryan would find the discovery interesting. When she entered her house, the telephone was ringing.

"Hello," she answered.

"Hello. Is this Emma Dennison?" The voice on the phone asked.

"Yes."

"This is Deputy Benish at the New Jericho Police Department. We have your husband here. He's been on somewhat of a bender and received a ticket for driving under the influence. He's currently in the drunk-tank and he is not a happy camper. I thought I should inform you that, if you come and make his bail, you can take him home."

"Thank you, Deputy. What if I don't want to take him home?"

"Well, it's Friday afternoon and the judge

has already left for the day. If his bail isn't made, he could be sitting here until Tuesday. He says he's a professor and has a class Monday."

"Did he also tell you he's a jerk?"

"No, Mrs. Dennison, he didn't tell me that."

"Well, he should have. I'm not sure what I am going to do, Deputy. I will give the matter some thought."

"All right then. We will just keep him where he is until you come for him or he goes before the judge, whichever comes first."

At that moment, Emma Dennison realized her marriage was finished. Like the collapse of the Twin Towers on 9/11, it would be a pivotal moment; one which she would always remember. There would be no more whining and complaining, no more demands for her husband to straighten up and reform himself. It was finished. Anything else that followed would be details only. The end was certain and inevitable.

Emma accepted this fact without remorse. She felt nothing—neither anger nor disappointment. She was empty inside—numb. All she knew was that she would have to alter her plans if she was to get on with the business of living the rest of her life in any meaningful way. She thought she might move to Texas and live with Ruthie and her family. As far as going to New Jericho to rescue her husband...again..., she decided against it. *Let him wait,* she thought. *Let him stew in his own juices. I'm tired of being his enabler.*

Jim Pahz

18

It was Friday afternoon, shortly after her conversation with the deputy, when Emma drove her car down the dirt road to Lilly's cottage. *Before I go to Texas or anywhere else, I'm going to confront that woman. I need some questions answered. If Lilly wants Ryan, she can have him. She can even go and get him out of jail. I couldn't care less.*

She parked the car and then saw an old woman about twenty yards away in front of the cottage. Her silver-gray hair hung down loosely over her shoulders. She was dressed in all black and stood in front of the easel painting. She reminded Emma of the bad witch in *The Wizard of Oz*. She wore everything but the pointy hat. The old woman turned and faced Emma. She looked confused and mean.

"I knew it was you," Emma said in a loud voice. "That girl is a liar. You're the artist, aren't you?"

"What did you think?" The old woman cackled. The sound of her voice sent chills up Emma's spine.

"I thought your eyes were bad—dimmed with old age. I didn't think you could see. To be honest, I thought you were too old to do most anything. You can barely walk by yourself."

"You'd be surprised the things I can do," the old woman hissed.

Emma heard a baby cry inside the cottage. It startled her. Without saying another word, she turned and ran to the door. It was an instinctive response; there was no thinking involved. She opened the door and stepped into the cottage. Although the light was dim, she immediately saw a playpen and within it stood a baby. It looked like... it was... baby Allison! Emma recognized her immediately. She scooped up her granddaughter and covered her with kisses. "Oh my sweet baby. Allison, is it you? You're alive! You're alive!" She examined the baby, smelled her aroma, and listened to her heartbeat. "It's a miracle. I'm taking you home," she said, heading for the door. "I'm not leaving you with that old crone."

As soon as she reached the threshold, she saw a snarling black wolf standing in front of the cottage. The hair on the back of the animal's neck was standing up and Emma saw saliva drip from its mouth. Emma slammed the door shut. "What do you want from me?" she screamed. "This baby isn't yours. She is mine. She is my granddaughter, Allison. She doesn't belong to you and you can't have her." Emma pressed her weight against the door to keep it from being forced open.

For a few moments there was quiet—no sounds whatsoever. Everything was completely still. No songbirds were heard, and even the wolf had stopped growling. Complete silence, and then Emma heard words in a very pleasant sing-song manner that sounded like a young girl.

The voice said, "Oh, all right. Have it your way. You can keep the baby on one condition. Please, open the door and come outside. We can visit. I would like that very much. I won't hurt you. I promise."

Slowly, Emma opened the door. When she peeked outside, where the wolf had been, now stood Lilly—the young Lilly, the one Emma had met that first time when she was with Ryan, the girl who spoke in riddles and acted like a half-wit. Now Lilly was smiling.

She looked as young and fresh as ever. She was the personification of loveliness and innocence.

"Where is the wolf?" Emma asked timidly.

"You're looking at her—different shape, same entity." The girl giggled. Then she growled like a wolf. "I can be anything I want."

"And the old lady?"

"Yeah.... her too." She laughed again. "You want me to show you?"

"No. Please don't."

"Then come out. That way I won't have to blow the house down like I did to that arrogant little piggy."

"Will I be safe? You won't hurt me? Can I really take my granddaughter and go? What is your condition?"

"Yes, you can, so please come out. I give you my word. I won't hurt a hair on your chinny chin chin. So come on out now and visit with me. Please...please."

Emma stepped out of the cottage and onto the porch. She was still holding Allison, and still trembling. She looked around for the wolf and for the old woman. They weren't anywhere to be seen.

In a soft voice, Emma inquired, "What are you?"

"I am Lilith."

"I know what your name is, but what does it mean?"

"It means…," Lilly looked thoughtful, "that I am the essence of boredom," She tossed her head shaking her hair as if it was wet and she was trying to dry it.

"Why?"

She appeared to be considering the question. "I don't know why. It just is. It's always been that way. Maybe because I've done all there is to do. I've done it again and again and I'm tired."

"What's wrong with doing things?"

"Nothing, at first. But try doing the same thing for a thousand years. Repetition makes things lose their appeal, and I mean everything."

"Nothing pleases you? Nothing makes you happy?"

"Some things. Painting pleases me. I enjoy painting. I've painted for a long time. It's one of the few things I do well. Talking to you pleases me. That's why I want to visit. Please stay awhile."

"Did you copy that painting in the Kunst Museum in Vienna?"

"No, of course not." She looked offended. "I don't copy, I create. All my art is original. I painted that picture. That's why my name is on it, or didn't you notice?" She spoke like a child, pouting.

"The book in the library said you painted it in 1733."

"Yes, but that was the second time. Originally I painted it around the year 1300, if I recall correctly. As I get older, I'm having more difficulty remembering things, especially details. The first version was burned in a fire along with a Knight Templar. Funny, I can't recall his name, but I remember he was a very serious-minded individual, and quite committed to his vocation. I liked him. The court of inquiry didn't. They said the painting was a product of witchcraft, so they burned it along with him. I think the second rendition is the one in the museum in Austria."

"How is it possible? How old are you?"

She paused to reflect. Then in a serious voice she answered, "Old enough—as old as the mountains. Let's just say, age doesn't apply to me. Not like it does to you or your kind. I've always been here. I imagine I always will be."

"What are you saying? Are you... a demon?"

"Oh, please." The expression on her face showed disappointment. "I hate that word. It is so... so pejorative. I prefer to think of myself as a supernatural malcontent." She smiled again, obviously pleased with her answer. "I am embittered, lonely, and misunderstood. But I'm not bad, not in the way you mean. I used to be, I confess, but not any more."

"Are you unique? I mean, are you the only one like you?"

"No, there are others—not many, but a few."

"Do you hang out together? Do you have a club, or a gang—something like that?"

"No, we shun each other's company. As a rule, we're not very likable. Some of us are terrible, others are worse. You heard about that shooting spree in the movie theater. Well, there you are—influence. We can have a bad effect on people."

"What about Allison? She was dead."

Emma held her granddaughter tightly and kissed her forehead.

"No, not really. She just looked dead. It was an illusion. Besides, I had help on the inside. Haven't you ever heard of zombies? It's a parlor trick I learned when I was in Haiti. Anybody can do it, if you have the right ingredients and a little help on the inside."

"Help on the inside? Do you mean the creepy looking fellow who drove the ambulance? Was he working with you?"

"Very perceptive. You're a bright girl."

"I'm not a girl, Lilly, I'm a grandmother. I haven't been a girl in a long time." She was talking down to Lilly like a grownup would talk to a child.

"Oh yes, that's right. Excuse me, you're the adult here." Lilly looked around like she was trying to remember something important. Then she said, "Age is relative. You do know that, don't you? It's not an alien concept? You look at me and see a young girl, but that is an illusion. I am old. Cross my heart and hope to die. Strike me dead if I should lie." She lapsed again in her giggly, childish voice. "But you can't strike me dead. That's the problem. Notwithstanding, compared to me, you are an infant."

"The creepy ambulance driver looked a little like Mr. Metcalf," Emma said. "Are they related?"

"They're brothers."

"Really?"

"No, not really. It's none of your beeswax."

"I'm sorry. I don't mean to pry. I know it's not my business, but when I was in the gallery one day I noticed Mr. Metcalf rub the back of his ear. Then he smelled his thumb. I saw him do it a few times."

"Disagreeable habit. Someone should speak to him about that."

"Why did you want Allison?"

"Company. I am lonely. Maybe I'm developing maternal instincts. Who knows? Metcalf is dull. He's soft-minded. Besides, after 300 years he's starting to fall apart."

"Is that why he rubs the back of he ear and smells it?"

"I suppose. I'm afraid, dear Metcalf is beginning to come unglued—literally. Maybe he's rotting?"

"That's disgusting."

"Yes, so you can see why I need someone new."

"What is Mr. Metcalf? Is he a relative of yours?"

"A relative?" Lilly started to giggle and then broke into laughter. "That's a good one. I guess you could say that. Metcalf is my golem. Didn't you realize that? I made him myself, out of clay and something like silly-putty and adhesive. Maybe you're not as perceptive as I thought. Metcalf has assisted me for 300 years. Believe me, he looked better when he was new. And he wasn't smelling his ear all the time. But I need a real person. Metcalf's time is growing short. His ear is only the first part starting to go."

"And that's why you wanted Allison?"

"No, I'm sorry, I don't want her now. I already told you. She's all yours. I said you can have her and I meant it. I always keep my word. I can find someone else. Babies are... how you people say, a dime a dozen. And if I can't find a baby, there are always runaways needing a home. Someone will become available. They always do. "

"What's to keep me from running to the authorities when I leave here?"

"Nothing." Lilly's voice changed again to serious. "Have at it. Be my guest. When the authorities come, they will find nothing. You will be regarded as a crazy person who wasted everybody's time. Likely, you will be institutionalized. Did you ever see that old film *The Snake Pit*? I believe it starred Olivia de Havilland. It's not a nice place to be—an insane asylum. But hey, it's a free country, do what you want."

Emma stopped to think. She didn't know how much of what Lilly was saying was true. It was too fantastic. Likely, Lilly herself belonged in the asylum. Yet Emma couldn't deny what she saw with her own eyes. She only knew she wanted to leave. "I need to go," she said. "I have things to do."

"Emma, wait a minute. Please. There's no need to get your panties in a bunch. I want you to be my friend." She was in her childlike, innocent voice again. "I admire your perseverance. It does you credit. I haven't met many people like you—people I respect. Stay for a while and talk with me. I don't get much company. Of course, there was one exception, the business with your husband. I admit to the indiscretion and I apologize. Honestly, I could hardly keep him away. He kept coming back and sniffing around here like he was a dog after a bitch in heat. Come to think of it, I haven't seen him for a while."

"He's incarcerated."

"Oh, well, that would explain it."

"Did you have an affair with my husband?"

"I don't know whether I would dignify it by calling it an affair. That involves some level of emotional commitment. But if you mean sex—did we sleep together? Of course. It was no big deal and I already apologized. What more can I say?"

Emma looked at Lilly. The girl was so effervescent and full of life. Emma smiled. "Looking at you, I can hardly blame him, or any man. You're incredibly beautiful. You literally are a person without a flaw; not a single blemish. It's amazing. And, as if that weren't enough, you have the blessing of youth. You're a rose in full bloom." Then Emma paused and looked critically at Lilly. "But I suspect you are aware of all that stuff. What I can't figure out is why choose Ryan?"

"Oh, Emma. It's what I do. It's what I've always done. I don't discriminate. Well, not much. I'm a seductress. I tempted Adam in the garden, but we didn't get along. I was a courtesan in Venice, a harem girl in Turkey, a geisha in Japan. I've known men like King Saul, Aristotle, Galilao, even your first president, George Washington. I was their inspiration—their muse. Ryan was just the latest to get in line. And believe me, Emma, it's a long line, and it includes some impressive names. Ryan might not rise to their level of achievement, but he's not a complete loser. After all, he is a professor, a scholar; that must account for something."

"Not much," Emma said. The conversation was so bizarre and unsettling, Emma wanted to run away. She wanted to take the baby and flee, to escape the nightmare. But Emma was a pragmatist, and she wasn't stupid. She wasn't going to do anything that might get Lilly angry with her or jeopardize the welfare of baby Allison. And then, in some strange way, she realized she actually felt sorry for Lilly. Emma could understand loneliness. And Lilly seemed so sweet and isolated.

"All right," Emma said, "I'll visit, but just for a little while. What is the condition you spoke of? I won't bargain for Allison.

You can't have her soul. I want to take her back to her mother and father in Texas. Do you have any idea how heartbroken they are? I was considering moving to Texas and living with them. I am divorcing Ryan. I've had it with his drinking, not to mention his philandering. That decision has already been made. You can have him if you want him."

"No, thank you. I like Texas, but it's too hot for me there. I prefer Michigan. In Michigan, you have a change of seasons. You're on the 45th parallel, and as far as global warming is concerned, Michigan is a good place to be. The growing season is getting longer, the winters are less severe, and there is plenty of fresh water. Water is going to become a precious resource in the future.

"Look, Emma, don't go to Texas. Stay here and live with me. I'm not a bad thing. Well, yes, I guess I am, maybe. I mean, you could say I was bad, in the past. But I'm not always bad. I'm not required to be bad—not all the time. I know I've done some terrible things, wicked things. I admit it. I mean, think about it. I've been around a long time. But it hasn't been all bad and I'm proud of some of the decisions I've made. I am my own person and take control. I refused to submit to my husband and be subservient. Not me. I wouldn't do what he expected of me because it wasn't what I wanted to do. All we did was bicker with one another. I grew sick of it, so I left him. Garden or no garden, I had enough and I walked out.

"I believe I was probably the first feminist. I'm proud of that. I never regretted leaving that Adam person. I stand by my decision. To be honest, I'm sick of sex. Not tonight dear—I have a headache. Not tonight or any other night. Not for a long time. Don't misunderstand me, Emma. I'm not saying that all men are dogs—although most of them are—but as far as men are concerned, I need some time off. I can use a vacation.

"I confess, I'm not pleased with some of my past behavior. But in the last few centuries, I've changed. I've become somewhat of a pacifist. I don't like killing. I used to enjoy it; I mean I'd really get off on pulling people's arms out, watching them writhe in agony, and seeing their blood spill. I went a little crazy during the plague years. Life was cheap then. I guess I was a bit overenthusiastic, but not anymore. I mean, I'm past all that. It's boring.

"I could kill you right now if I wanted to, but I don't. I'd much rather talk and be friends. The company of friends is important to me, Emma, and I don't have many. Actually, to be truthful, I don't have any. I had a friend once. Solomon. We used to try and stump one another by thinking up riddles. It was fun, but it was a long ago. That's why I'm turning to you. I'm hoping you will permit me to be your friend. I need a buddy—a pal. Someone I can confide in; someone I can respect. You don't have tattoos, and that's a big plus."

"What difference does it make if I have tattoos or not? Ryan says most of his students have tattoos. He says body art is fashionable and popular with the students."

"Body art? Is that what you call it? I hate it. Old people don't like tattoos, and I am old—remember?"

"Why?"

"Why am I old?"

"No. Why don't you like tattoos?"

"I don't know. They don't appeal to me. They're ugly. As time passes they get uglier. The ink blurs and runs together. I think an old person looks ridiculous with tattoos. Besides, there is a direct relationship between tattoos and how easily a person is influenced. I remember this from my younger days, before I changed my ways and wasn't the best influence on people. If I saw a person covered with ink, I knew I was dealing with an impressionable and insecure individual—a person with a soft mind. Such a person is an easy mark."

"That may have once been true, but not today. Things change, you know."

"Tell me about it! But some things never change. I don't change—well, not entirely. My attitude may change, but I, myself, don't change. Besides, ugly is ugly. Did you ever see one of these people who are covered in tattoos? They look all blue and green, like some sort of amphibian, something that crawled out from under a rock. To me, a tattoo signifies identification, but in a negative way. Slaves were marked with tattoos in Rome, as were criminals and gladiators. These were people who weren't free. They belonged to someone else. When the Nazis ran the concentration camps, they marked their victims with tattoos. They weren't applying 'body art.' They were marking people for extermination. To me, tattoos have always been associated with unpleasant memories and unsavory characters."

"That may have been true in the past. Today things are different. Most people have only one or two tastefully done tattoos."

"There is no such thing as a tastefully done tattoo, Emma. That is an oxymoron."

"You know, Lilly, you're very opinionated for an individual who has been around for as long as you say you have. I would think you might have mellowed a bit with age. You could be a little more tolerant."

"Tolerance—that's a buzzword for the modern age. Maybe I should have some diversity training." Lilly giggled. "You can take tolerance, Emma, and stick it where the sun don't shine—if you get my drift. I prefer the Popeye philosophy: 'I yam what I yam.' Nevertheless, I respect your ideas and will consider your words.

"These days, I prefer harmony over chaos and disorder. I prefer the company of nice people, like you, people without tattoos." She paused for a moment to reflect and then said, "I really did smell the fear when we met that time in the forest." Lilly smiled and giggled. "I'm sorry I frightened you. I feel bad about the whole peeing thing. And those boys, you don't seriously think they could have made a difference? Oh please! They were children!

"You know, lately I've become interested in environmental issues. I mean, if mankind doesn't alter the way he's treating the earth, what will we have? The seas are polluted. The fish are dying. There is a huge mass of sludge, larger than the continental United States, and it's just floating around the Pacific Ocean—a giant mega-patch of garbage. What I am saying is, I believe mankind can do better."

Emma was trying to be polite and stay attentive. She found that, although frightened, she actually liked Lilly, whom Emma saw as intriguingly candid. But she was wary. *This is the most bizarre conversation I've ever had. I must be dreaming. Why don't I wake up? But in case I'm not asleep, I better be very careful.* Then Emma asked, "So, you're not evil?"

"No, Emma. I don't think so." She

paused to reflect again. "I've had my moments, but it wasn't me who set fire to that Knight Templar. I didn't participate in the Inquisition or orchestrate the Auto-de-fé. I didn't burn all those poor old women throughout the ages. Remember Salem? That was right here in Massachusetts. I didn't support the Nazi movement in Germany, or cause the Holocaust and the death of six million Jews. I could go on and on—the Turks and Armenians, the Cherokee trail of tears, the Khmer Rouge and the killing fields of Cambodia, the genocide in Darfur. I think you get my point.

"The world doesn't need me to cause mayhem; man is quite capable of destroying himself without any help from me. And yes, Emma, there is evil in the world; there always has been, and there always will be. But I am not the culprit. I am a bystander. I have a job to do, like a snapping turtle has a job to do in a pond. I have a role to play in the universe, and I do my job.

"But my interests have changed. I don't want to do demonic things anymore. There's that word, *demon*, again. I hate that word. Maybe I've just been around for too long, maybe I've seen too many movies. I'm tired of being the villain. I want to put on a white hat and be the good guy for a change. Whichever god created me will have to reassess what he or she envisioned as my role in the universe. It will be necessary to change my job description, because I am not doing that stuff anymore. I'm just not cooperating. I quit. So there you have it.

"Except now, I've broken a rule. I'm not supposed to reveal myself—oops!"

She sounded like a teenager and reminded Emma of her daughters when they were teens.

"So I will have to leave, get out of town, skedaddle, head for the hills. I appreciate having had the opportunity to unburden myself. You've been a good listener, Emma, and I thank you. I've kept all this stuff bottled inside of me for so long. I just wanted to talk to somebody and let it out. But okay, now I've done that. I've had my cathartic release—my temper tantrum. We've reached the end of a delightful visit. So here is my condition. No, I'm not going to insist on conditions. I take that word back. I really am trying to change. Here is my *request*. Come and live with me and be my friend."

"Are you asking me to become your familiar or something creepy like that?"

"No, Emma, nothing like that. No familiars, no golems—just my friend. I want someone to talk with. I want companionship. I want to be able to share things. You go to Texas and visit with your family. Take the baby with you. Turn her over to her parents. You'll figure out some way to explain everything. You're clever. Stay a couple of months. Have a nice visit. My request is that you return and stay with me for the rest of the year. And Emma, I will sweeten the deal.

"Make a commitment to stay with me for two years, and I will release you from our agreement. At that time you will be free to go wherever you want without any interference from me. Who knows, after two years we might be like an old married couple. We might be cranky and have nothing left to say to one another. I'm trying to be fair, Emma. I'm not asking for the moon, just a two-year commitment."

"And if I refuse?"

"If you refuse...." Lilly paused and gave it some thought. "Then you'll refuse. There are no conditions to this request. In the past, I might have flown into a rage and pulled your arms off or disemboweled you. I had anger management issues then. But, as I've said, I've changed. You can take the baby and go. But, if that is your choice, then as far as you're concerned, I never existed. I wasn't here and we never had this conversation. You must keep it a secret. There are rules. Even if I don't agree with them, I still must obey them.

"I've enjoyed our afternoon together, Emma. You are good company. You're a level-headed grandma. You don't panic, or act stupid. That is an admirable quality, Emma. And you don't have tattoos. I hope we can be friends. If you don't commit to me, I hope you will think of me once in a while, and in a favorable way. Not like in all the books on mythology with the nonsense about how I live in a cave and strangle babies. I'm not like that. You've seen my house. Isn't it cute? I like decorating. My favorite channel is the *Home and Garden Network*. I believe I could be a *Design Star*. And as for strangling babies, I haven't strangled a baby in 300 years!

"I will be leaving this place. I'm not going to Texas, but I'm going somewhere. It's time to make changes. If you bring people here and tell others to search for me, with or without pitch forks, they won't find me. They won't even find my owls. I'm taking them with me. They will find only a run-down, abandoned house. Trust me on this, Emma, I don't lie. I keep my word. Take your granddaughter to Texas. In six months time, I will contact you. But you are under no obligation. The choice is yours."

Emma felt a swelling of gratitude. "Thank you Lilly, for permitting me to take my granddaughter. Thank you for allowing me to leave. Thank you for not killing me. I will remember you fondly, as my friend. Wherever I go, I will keep the memory of you alive. You are a great painter, Lilly, the best one I know, and the best one I will ever know. I am positive about that."

Lilly walked over to Emma and gave her an embrace. Her touch was cold and it made Emma feel chilled. "Think about my offer, my friend. Go on, Emma. Take your granddaughter home with you. Take her to her mother, before I change my mind and peel your skin off and feed it to the crows. Remember the story of the scorpion and the frog?"

Suddenly, Emma was frozen in terror. She wanted to run, but her legs wouldn't move.

"Just kidding, Emma. Don't wet yourself, again. I'm not a scorpion. Do I look like a scorpion? Even supernatural malcontents can have a sense of humor. Life is hard. There's so much misery in the world, one needs to be able to laugh. Otherwise, we'd all go nuts." She smiled a wide smile. Then, in her sing-song, childish voice she said, "Go on, Emma, get out of here."

Emma calmly walked to the car and placed Allison in the back seat. She got into the driver's seat and began to drive down the two-track. She let out a sigh of relief, glad to have the bizarre episode behind her. "Thank God," she said out loud. Then she glanced in her rearview mirror and saw something remarkable. It was a stag. It raised and lowered its head as if nodding in the affirmative. It wasn't necessary to count the points on its antlers. "Goodbye, Lilly," Emma said. She wondered what she would decide to do.

Jim Pahz

19

Emma sat at the table in the kitchen of her one-bedroom apartment. The table was old. It was made from polished steel with a Formica surface. Emma guessed it was in vogue sometime around the 1950s, but that was a long time ago. She had purchased the table and chairs from the Salvation Army Thrift Shop. It was cheap and something about it reminded Emma of when she was a little girl. *Shabby chic*, Emma thought, *or just plain ugly. Take your pick. The colors are awful—green and gray. Depressing. Maybe that's why I like it; it suits me.*

Emma had left Ryan right after he was released from jail. There was nothing left to say or do. She refused marriage counseling, and even though Ryan cried and pleaded she remained firm. "We've been through all of this before, Ryan. You're not going to change and you're not going to stop drinking. My mind is made up and I've already retained an attorney. There's nothing more to discuss. Get a grip on yourself. The homestead is yours, all eighty acres. I don't want any part of it. I'm moving to town while I get my life straightened out."

Now, sitting at her obnoxious table, she reflected on her latest adventure. She had to smile when she thought about how devious she was in returning Ruthie's baby to her and Michael. Emma had employed an elaborate ruse that was complicated and costly. It involved hiring an actor to impersonate a police officer. He explained about a woman who had kidnapped Allison and switched babies at the hospital. The woman's baby had been terminally ill and the poor individual, overcome with grief, had acted out of impulse and desperation. The crime was solved and the right baby returned to Emma. The distraught woman was declared mentally incompetent, and sent to a mental health facility. It had really been the crazy woman's baby that was buried.

Of course, none of the story was true. It was a bogus tap dance, and Emma was surprised she was able to get away with it. But as Lilly said, Emma was a clever girl. Ruthie and Michael were so overjoyed with happiness from having Allison back in the family that they hardly questioned anything about the outrageous story. Emma reasoned that people hear what they want to hear. Ruthie and Michael would have believed anything, even if Emma told them she found Allison growing from a bean stalk in the garden. They would have believed—because they wanted to believe. Emma felt that the matter of Allison was finally finished. Allison was back where she belonged.

But now a bigger problem loomed on the horizon. She would be contacted soon by Lilly, and what was Emma going to do? It was a storm cloud on the horizon. *Who am I?* She thought. *Do I want to be a demon's disciple? Is this the best I can hope for?*

Emma had never been a religious person. But she had always been a woman of principle. And she was filled with platitudes. How many times had she admonished her daughters by saying things like, "Never sacrifice the future on the altar of the immediate;" or, "Haste makes waste;" or, "Birds of a feather flock together." They were easy phrases to remember, and folksy wisdom which might have done her children some good. Now, those words made Emma feel like a hypocrite.

But she was intrigued by Lilly. That couldn't be denied. She didn't believe all the talk about how Lilly wasn't bad anymore; how she had changed. Bullshit! Emma knew better. Lilly did, after all, kidnap Allison. That behavior was inexcusable. It certainly wasn't the behavior of a person who was once bad, but now good. Oh no. Taking Allison was evil—pure and simple. And being lonely and wanting a companion was no excuse. Lilly hadn't changed that much. And she did lure Emma's husband away.

Still, when all was said and done, Emma was drawn to Lilly. *Like a moth to a flame. Now that,* she told herself, *is a dilemma. What to do?* Maybe she should talk to somebody, a psychologist or cleric; someone who could give advice. But then she reasoned, *who is going to believe me? If I tell a psychiatrist he is going to say I'm delusional and lock me up. If I talk to a cleric, they're going to tell me to get away—avoid the demon at all cost. Run as fast as I can. You never invite a demon into your life. Everybody knows that.*

So what will I do? Lilly had promised she would require only a two-year commitment. *Two years is nothing. It will pass in no time.*

So, I have an escape clause—a way out. And, I would like to travel. I would like that very much. A line popped into Emma's head, *"Oh, the things that you'll do, the places you'll see."* Who said that? She thought maybe it was Dr. Seuss, or some other children's book writer. It was something from the time her children were small and she used to read aloud to them. But they weren't small now. They were all grown up, and Emma had no one to read to. She was alone—by herself; and truth was that, Emma was lonely—just like Lilly. *I can look at this situation as a glass half full, or half empty. The choice is mine.*

Yes, Emma thought, *I have a dilemma.* Emma knew she would have to make a decision. Six months had almost passed. She would be visited soon.

Jim Pahz

20

Allison is fifteen years old today. She has no memory of ever being kidnapped or her time with Lilly. Her grandmother, Emma, has just had her sixty-fifth birthday. She came to visit and they had a grand party. This year, Granny-M, as Allison calls her grandmother, spent two months with Allison's family. It was during the winter months because in Michigan it's too cold for Emma.

Emma loves to travels. She has been just about everywhere there is worth seeing. She's been to Europe a couple of times; in Israel she worked on a kibbutz and in India, she lived in an ashram. She's seen most of the world's wonders, including the pyramids in Egypt, the Great Wall of China, Ayers Rock in Australia, and Angel Falls in Venezuela. Emma loves to travel. She says it's her favorite activity. She has a friend who accompanies her, a single lady about the same age as Emma. They're almost inseparable, and Emma describes Miss Lilly as her best friend. She is a lovely woman, elegant and sophisticated. Men turn their heads whenever Miss Lilly walks by. Emma says men are silly.

Jamie still lives in Michigan. She never married. Jamie is a hard worker and very level-headed. She began her career as a real estate salesperson and worked her way up. She recently obtained her broker's license, and these days, she heads her own agency, called *Home Sweet Home*. Jamie moved from New Jericho and relocated to Mount Pleasant, Michigan. She says there is more opportunity there, with the casino and new medical school, and a regional hospital center.

It's been more than a decade since anyone's heard from or about Ryan. When he got out of jail he started drinking again. He had another mishap with the law. This time it was serious. It involved the death of a college student. Ryan was convicted of vehicular homicide and sentenced to a term in prison. The incident occurred right after Emma obtained her divorce. As far as the family is concerned, Ryan just fell off the grid. The family doesn't talk about him. Everyone assumes Ryan is alive, but nobody really knows, and nobody makes any effort to look for him. The family has accepted the reality of Ryan's situation. Addiction is a terrible disease.

Jim Pahz

EPILOGUE

They allow him to keep a box under his cot. It's just a plain cardboard box he obtained from a grocery store. Inside the box is a change of underwear, his toothbrush, and his Ph.D. These days the diploma is not doing him much good. It's the last thing he hasn't pawned, but he might. Every day he goes out and scrounges for a few dollars. When he has enough, he buys liquor. Sometimes he can't get a bed at the shelter, if he gets there too late in the evening and there is no vacancy. In that case, he hides his box and sleeps under a blue tarp beneath a bridge. It can get awfully cold in Michigan, especially in winters. Sometimes he thinks he might freeze to death.

When he was released from jail the first time, he didn't go home. Instead he went straight to the cottage in the woods. It was deserted. He couldn't understand what had happened to it. The house looked like it had been abandoned for ages. The structure was decaying and falling apart. Even the owl sentries had been removed. Vandalism. A short time later he was arrested again for driving while intoxicated. This time he was involved in a hit-and-run. He should have remained at the scene of the accident, but he didn't. He panicked and ran away. He took the coward's way out. The result was he was arrested, tried, and convicted. He was incarcerated for a long time. In prison, he had lots of time to think. When Ryan was finally released, he moved in for a while with his brother, Doug. That didn't work out because Ryan couldn't stop drinking. Eventually Doug asked him to leave. He said he didn't want his grandchildren exposed to Ryan's behavior.

***

These days Ryan sometimes catches a glimpse of her. But he can't really be sure. It could be the alcohol, or maybe it's just wishful thinking. He believes he saw her last fall when her black hair was blown all crazy-like in a cool breeze. She looked terrific. Once he saw her dressed as a professional woman, in a business suit, with her hair up, and wearing eyeglasses. He was on a street corner, panhandling. Fortunately, she didn't see him, because he would have been embarrassed.

He thinks about her often. He has seen her in many places and disguises, at many different times. He believes this, but he can't really be certain. Yesterday he thought he saw a musk ox and three dead monkeys by the side of the road. The mind plays tricks on people.

She told him once there would be a price to pay for his pleasure. Ryan figures he's paid the price and then some. That price was the life of his granddaughter—poor little Allison—not to mention the loss of his job and family. He knows the whole episode was his fault. There is no one else to blame. He was a weak man. He still is. That's why he fled the accident. That's why *he lives in a bottle*. Nobody held a gun to his head and forced him to drink.

Besides, he lusted after that girl, and he takes full responsibility for the consequences. Ryan believes Lilly is a demon. He didn't believe that when he knew her, but he came to that conclusion while in prison. He doesn't believe she's the only one. Ryan knows there are more. The world must be full of demons; some are bad and others are worse. They torment him at night and keep him from sleeping. So he drinks. His excuse is—demons or insomnia. Take your pick. He knows he'll eventually pass out, and when he's unconscious, then he will dream. It's always the same dream, the one about her—the temptress. She offered the most wonderful pleasure he has ever known. And, although he has trouble these days remembering things, he will always remember her.

For a brief time he basked in her radiance—the ecstasy of Lilith. He feels he doesn't need to remember anything more: her memory and a bottle of scotch whiskey are all he needs.

The End

Lilith